Gay erotic male bonding at its best.

Welcome to Hephaestion's world. Twenty-three centuries ago the second most powerful man in the world chose life as a vampire to the uncertainty of death. His lover was none other than Alexander the Great. Legend has it that they were one soul inhabiting two bodies. Before Eternity, Volume One introduces the reader to the whimsical vampire, as he introduces the writer of his chronicles (the little known Stefan Pride), his friends in present day Boston, and recounts his life with Alexander, before he was turned into an immortal by the mysterious Quermen.

Inflicted with AADD, his narration is at times historically accurate, often funny, sporadically sad, and peppered with some of the most visual inspiring erotic stories to ever disgrace a page.

READER ADVISORY

Please be advised that this book contains exclusively gay themed material and presents homosexual male to male (s) sex, which is very descriptive in its erotic nature. The content of this book is meant to be purchased and read only by persons eighteen years of age and older.

ISBN: 978-0-615-55496-9

CONTENTS

Acknowledgement

It is with great pleasure that I give my sincere thanks to Marco, who created not only the beautiful art representing Alexander the Great and Hephaestion, but actually designed the book cover for Before Eternity, vol. I. Marco had requested that if I remarked about the cover art at all, that I limit it to only a few lines. But I couldn't find it in me to do that. Please forgive me Marco.

I can only hope that the interior of the book gives as much pleasure as the visual made possible by this artist's talent. My friend Marco was born in Florence, Italy in 1966. Throughout his life he always tried to find beauty in everything around him and mainly in the male figure. He prefers to represent the male nude as the man next door, but also as a dream. His belief that the masculine figure can hide a sensual poetry is represented in the beauty and strength expressed through his depiction of the male form. He and his boyfriend live in a quiet country house between Florence and Arezzo, Italy.

I strongly recommend that you visit his fantastic gallery at www.artimarkz.com to explore more of his work. Thank you Marco.

PROLOGUE

Hello, my name is Hephaestion and I am a vampire. Forgive me that this, my first attempt to pen a memory to written form, is so poorly achieved. While it is true that I have had centuries... I am exaggerating the memory already. Vanity has always been a flaw of mine. Let's start over shall we? While it is true that I have had millennia to write the story of my life (there I go again)...my death, there have been just as many distractions. I have had, you see, a very busy death. In fact so busy has my death been I often forget that I am not one of the living. It has been one as vibrantly full and robust as my short life. However, because no concise history has ever been written about me, I feel the need to set the record straight.

I have chosen to write this story in modern vernacular. If I had decided to share my story five hundred years ago I no doubt would have done it in the language of Shakespeare. If I retell it five hundred years from now then it will be in the language spoken then. Though I can't imagine this language becoming any more defiled than it already has. Oh well! With that said let me begin.

I had been thinking for centuries that I should keep a journal. Not to refresh my own memory because everything I have ever done or said is in my memory word for word. It is just that now the time feels right for me to share. Some of you will believe my story while others will laugh and call me a liar. It is of little matter to me. What is important is that I give the world my history, do with it what you will.

I have also decided to use a journalist, who is a young newcomer, as my ghostwriter. One reason is I have taken a liking to him but most importantly he will keep me from wondering too far off the topic...I hope. How my commerce with this writer began will be introduced to you shortly. His name is Stefan Pride and he will be given credit for writing this and all future recounts of my history, even though they are written in the first person. The parts involving his interview to work for me are actually by yours truly because he becomes uncomfortable when speaking of himself. He was a hard one to convince but as you will see, he did come to realize the rewards of working for me.

I hope you can enjoy some of my life in its story form as much as I have enjoyed living it.

Chapter One
My Life Today and the People in It

Where do I start to tell a tale so fantastic that even I have difficulty believing some of it actually happened in that lifetime so long ago? At the beginning might be the best and once I have established my birth, my youth, some indiscretions (for reader interest only, of course), my most untimely death, and my resurrection to your satisfaction, I should then be free to skip around the centuries, if I so choose. It is unfortunate that while my resurrection gave me my immortality (or at least I suppose I can live forever. I won't actually know until I have...but that is an oxymoron isn't it?), my permanent youth (one might think that thirty-two is stretching the word youth, but indulge me I had always appeared younger than my years), my ability to bring any man and most women (cold vipers that most may be) into lust and adoration, my vampirism did not cure my wandering mind. Today it is known as AADD (Adult Attention Deficit Disorder). I was always afflicted with a "noisy:" mind. That's the awful truth. Case in point, not only am I a vampire, but I am a vampire who can have my cock sleeved in the tight ass of a beautiful young athlete and thinking of nothing but filling him with my vampiric little swimmers...my cock expands in his ass and I am ready to explode. Then, in a blink of an eye my mind goes from intense shagging to the upcoming Milan fashion show. Or more likely to a brief moment of passion that happened thousands of years ago in another reality. Just like that! I orgasm none-the-less, even if I'm not mentally present. The athlete intuitively feels my mental absence. Not caring, he still moans and cums without touching himself. He's pleased. I'm angry that I lost this experience to a memory. What do I do? Do I take my frustration out on this very straight boy, kiss his neck and drain him so there will be no talk of my inattentive performance? No, that would be a crime against nature. His ass is way too tight and those beautifully arched Italian lips way too good at doing what God meant them to do. I give him a memory plant of a buxom blonde rugby fan who seduced him into plowing her wet fetid pussy with its slimy folds (I had to throw that in just to cause my mortal sperm receptacle a bit of sexual confusion). I feed from inside his hairless thigh, his silky ball sac soft against my cheek, before leaving him in his cluttered little dorm room, with its posters of young girls with big tits. Tits that in all too short a time will be stretch marked and pendulous. I am gone. I am only a shadow memory somewhere in his dream state. When he awakens he will wonder why he is so tired and why his asshole is so sore. Then he will go about his day. One thing is for certain; never again will he look at his comrades showering in the locker room without a worrisome thought of what it would be like to share seed with them. Perhaps I will look him up again, I think, as my shiny red Lamborghini makes its way down the drive and out the college gates. Well, chalk up another memory I think; still tasting the sexual hormones released into his blood as I fucked him. But I regress. Enough of what I did for dinner tonight.

So there is no confusion, I think I should confine this narrative to my mortal story (with the exception of course regarding my writer's introduction) in which I will include the events, the people, and my life choices that are the foundation of the person and ultimately the vampire I am today. Then, down the road perhaps, if my mortal readers and some of my more curious vampire brothers want to be told more of how I have entertained myself over the past twenty-five hundred years you will get word to me. As mentioned in my prologue, I have worked out a "situation" with a young up and coming author by the name of Stefan Pride to be my go-between. I probably could have written this faster myself without Stefan but he needs the work and quite frankly he annoyingly interrupts me at times to ask relevant questions. As a result I think he will lend a more human interest to the whole thing.

At first Stefan was reluctant to be my assistant, thinking me quite crazy. I offered him lodging free of charge in any of my homes in which I happened to be living. I stated a salary that will surpass his income as a journalist when he graduates college. I promised a full scholarship for his Harvard tuition for the next three years. Can you believe even after that he said that unless I could prove to him that I am, in fact a vampire and not a schizophrenic that he wanted nothing to do with me. I must tell you that I have always loved a challenge. I know that I could have hired any number of starving students who would have written anything I ask even if they didn't believe what they were putting to paper (or into Office Word as it were) but they weren't Stefan Pride. Nor do many humans possess Stefan's integrity. Stefan Pride, you see, is one of those rare human beauties that you keep thinking about him days after having just met him. He is one of those creations from the divine that if you were introduced to him at an office party and five minutes later he was gone his face is the one that would come back to you twenty years from now when asked what your idea of a perfectly formed man is. Believe me, I have seen some beautiful men over the last few thousand years and Stefan can certainly be counted among them. As important (almost) is the fact that he is brilliant. Most of the time he can actually keep up with my vampire mind and my

AADD. What more could I ask for than a beautiful face and an outstanding body that can converse with me without too many mindplants. Sometimes mindplants are necessary if I am trying to convey a thought that has no reference point in this era. Also, for some reason, it was important to me that Stefan agree to do this on his own and not from my controlling him.

"Ok Stefan. I will play along with you. What can I do to prove to you I am a vampire and not just some rich young eccentric?" I asked him point blank as we walked along Boston's waterfront, where he had agreed to meet me. "I could tell you of this very waterfront that we are walking by and how well I remember the hustle and bustle of men unloading the whaling ships of the precious oil drained from thousands of those magnificent creatures. That would have been in the 1850's.

Or I can tell you of my first trip here in a filthy little sail ship that creaked and swayed so much in the storms we came through to get here, that I thought my immortality would truly be tested as the waves all but swallowed us. I could describe to you the forest that stood here just on the other side of that parking lot and the poor fort and shanty town that was then Boston. Or perhaps you would like to hear about the young man, Jedediah. He was a youth of barely eighteen, whom I gave pleasure to even as I sipped his warm blood. He was such a delight and a total innocent. He did not know that it was even possible to receive a cock in that fashion. We actually became fast friends. I attended his wedding to a comely young lady and later learned that four of his seven children reached adulthood. Many years later I returned from civilization (Europe) and sat at Jedediah's bedside as his doctor. His had been a successful life as a merchant as a result of my funding his education. Now in old age he had suffered a massive stroke and found speech difficult, but he recognized me none-the-less. He tried to smile but I could read the confusion in his mind. He was wondering how the man fourteen years older than himself and whose seed he had swallowed countless times still looked to be in his late twenties. My sweet Jedediah, now a wisp of a man, had lived a long life.

"How long has it been my friend since we hid in the woods and did things the Bible forbade us do but that our nature condoned?" Jedediah thought to me.

"My ever sweet little love," I thought back to him; all the while holding his hand. "It seems but an hour since we ran and hid in those woods far from the scrutiny of prying eyes. I still remember the touch of your skin when I undressed you fully that first time. You were shaking so badly, that at first, I thought my senses of what you lusted for had deceived me."

"No you were not wrong. Everything in me wanted you; at the same time everything in me was telling me that it was wrong. But it wasn't was it?" Jedediah thought to me.

"No my love it was not wrong. Everything about it was right," I shot back to him.

Suddenly he was looking and acting agitated. His family standing around the bed grew concerned. I quickly planted a soothing thought to him and he relaxed his body. "Then why am I like this and you are as you are?" Jedediah's mind cried to mine.

"Because my love you belonged in your time. We had our time together. It was brief but it defined you. Look around this room at your children. They truly love you and had you come with me you would have cheated them out of their existence." I explained as soothingly as possible.

"How long since we lay together?" he wondered.

"It's been eighty years Jedediah. But as I said I remember it as if I had just pulled my staff out of you." I told him truthfully.

"A long time my old friend for me. I have missed you." A tear was forming at the corner of his eye.

"I have missed you Jedediah." Again Jedediah winced. "The pain is unbearable. Can you help me feel happiness one more time?" my old friend's eyes and mind pleaded to me. As his doctor I leaned over him after reassuring the family that his pain was leaving him. I locked his aged watering eyes with mine and pushed in the memory of our last coupling. It had been slow and deep, fast and loud, with every back and forth thrust my cap was nudging the nut of his prostate. Jedediah was feeling it. In my mind's eye I was seeing him as the youth he had been, with me covering his body and his ankles locked behind my back as he pushed up to take even more of me into his receiver. Just as on that actual day he was feeling his nuts contract up into his body as his generous prick began to spew ropes of young healthy sperm onto both our stomachs while he felt the fullness of my cock as it gushed, filling his insides. Our gaze was broken, Jedediah's eyes had closed and he looked at peace.

"The drug has taken hold," I told his family, who had no idea what had just transpired. "Let him sleep," I ordered them as I left the house to the smell of coal in the air and the sputter of horseless carriages. Indeed, Jedediah had lived long and witnessed much as this new age moved upon him. I knew that he would lie in a deep sleep upon his bed and never reawaken. He would live perhaps another hour in the afterglow of the sex we had just shared. I wondered in passing if the mortician who washed his withered old body for burial would actually realize what the fluid drying on his abdomen really was.

"You could tell me stories like this all night I'm sure. Storytelling and knowledge of history does not prove that you are a vampire. I don't even know why I am having this conversation. I should be working out with my rowing team even as we speak. Besides, we're out here walking in the daylight so you should have burst into flames about an hour ago shouldn't you have?" Stefan had truly brought me out of my memory room and was making light of me.

"Stefan, I believe I told you that the light thing is a myth." I responded to him somewhat miffed. "So tell me what can I do? But let's not talk out here any longer. Come to my house with me and let's sit down and I will answer any question you want but I will prove that I am what I say. Quite frankly in all my days I have never had to prove to anyone that I am what I am. This should be interesting."

"Ok. I will come to your house. I will give you an hour to prove to me you are what you say." With that Stefan followed me to my black and silver Bentley and to my house we drove. I decided to take him to my country estate rather than my penthouse in downtown Boston. This house is about thirty miles north of the city and sits on a very private couple of hundred acres. It had originally been built by one of the old robber barons in the late eighteen hundreds. It sits on a cliff high over the Atlantic, but has a stairway to the base of the cliff where there is a nice private beach. The house itself is enormous befitting the ego of the man who built it as well as the one who now owns it. The walls are of imported granite blocks of no less than four feet square. One enters the front of the house through bronze doors weighing two tons that are so balanced that a child's push can open them with ease. This leads into an enormous entryway with an enormous stairway at the end of the room. If you continue walking east beyond the stairs you will find yourself in a great garden room facing the sea, which is far below. Beyond that room, is a wide veranda of thirty feet wide stretching the distance of the house and having steps that lead to a formal garden ending at the cliff's edge.

I had chosen to take Stefan to this house in hopes of not only impressing him (in honesty, I had begun to realize he is not easily impressed by things) but because the drive through Boston's traffic and then the quiet countryside to Pella's Head (I named my house after a city which held many memories for me) would give us the chance to know each other better.

"So Stefan, tell me a little about you," I said in my best casual manner.

"Not much to tell to a person like you Mr. Alexander."

"Nonsense! All I will be talking about to you is me, hopefully. Also, Stefan, please call me Harry. It will both please me that you call me what a friend would and it will make it easier for me to talk to you." I entreated him. "I would truly like a synopsis of you in your own words."

Stefan sighed and decided to go along with my request. Probably since he was stuck in the car with me and just maybe he was warming to me a bit, he began to share some of his story.

"I was born in a small town in Indiana but ended up in a steel town in Ohio after my parents divorced when I was quite young. My mother remarried as had my father. Initially I was not a good student because I was really an unhappy kid and it showed. I didn't make friends easily and had little use for anyone. By the time I was in high school I came out of my shell. To the surprise of everyone I became a straight 'A' student. I had discovered that by throwing myself into academics I could escape an extremely unhappy home life. I am not much of a team player but I found it necessary to fake being one if I wanted academic recognition and scholarship. I would have done anything; I mean anything to get away from that home. I mean I loved my mother and knew she had sacrificed a lot for me and my brother, but I hated every moment I lived with that egotistical monster she had brought into our lives. I was able to escape the fear of that household through writing and fantasizing that I was another person somewhere else.   Something Mr. Alexa...Harry, I think you are doing now. I knew I was different but I knew I wanted more. So here I am trying to pay for an Ivy League college and become a famous journalist. What do I get? I get someone claiming to be a vampire asking for my help. Go figure man!"

"Well I'm not as bad as all that Stefan. So don't use your name if you don't want." I scolded him. "What do you mean you knew you were different?"
Stefan looked uncomfortable but then shrugged his broad shoulders and half smiled. "I don't bother to hide it from most people anymore. I'm as gay as you are. But then you already had that figured didn't you?"

By now we had pulled into the gates of the long drive to the house and made our way around the curves to suddenly find the mansion in front of us. "Holy fuck!" was all Stefan said as I pulled to the front of the house and a handsome young man with hair the color of straw and dressed only in shorts, sandals, and tank top ran to my door opening it for me. "Welcome home Mr. Alexander! Word was that you were staying in town."

"Thank you Todd. I have a guest who hopefully will be spending some time here working for me as a sort of secretary." I told the smiling young man. "Todd, I would like you to meet Mr. Stefan Pride. I am depending on you and the other boys to do anything you can to make Mr. Pride feel a part of our house."

"Oh yesss sir, Mr. Alexander. I am pleased to meet you Mr. Pride. Just let me know if you need anything." Todd told Stefan.

"I'm pleased to meet you Todd. But I think I will only be here for a couple of hours. But thanks man."

"Todd, how is your art coming? I'm anxious to see it when you have your showing in the city." I said to Todd as he slid behind the wheel of my car preparing to garage it.

"Sure thing, Mr. Alexander. I wouldn't even want anyone to see it if you weren't there." With that a beaming Todd was driving away
.

"Who was that?" Stefan inquired watching the vanishing Bentley.

"Todd does odd jobs around here in return for a place to stay and practice his painting. He is quite gifted and someday I will be able to look at his work long after his time and remember that I was a small help to him." I explained.

Stefan rolled his eyes. "There you go again. Just when I'm thinking that maybe you are a nice normal guy. Let's get this interview over with so you will be satisfied that I listened to you and so I'll be satisfied you won't harass me anymore."

"Oh Stefan, my boy! How times have changed. Soon enough you will know that men, even men as beautiful as you, have met unimaginable fates for saying less than you have to me today. I wasn't always this nice you know." I laughed putting my arm around his shoulders and guiding him into my house.

We were met at the door by a dark haired beauty of a man. His shiny black hair was shoulder length and trimmed in such a way that he had a disarming way of moving his head to keep it out of eyes the color of deep sapphires. Only when the light hit those orbs with their thick long lashes could one see that they were indeed blue and not ebony. His lips were full and luscious, if not a bit pouty. He wore a heavy five o'clock shadow regardless of how often he shaved. Like Todd he was about twenty-one and he wore sandals, shorts, and a tank top. Unlike Todd, who had the complexion of cream and the smooth legs and chest of a boy several years his junior, this young man had a light dusting of black hair on his legs as well as on his chest.

"Mr. Alexander, sir. We were not expecting you home until later in the month. Welcome home! I am so happy to see you." The young man said in what was an unmistakable New England accent. His face was literally shining he was so happy to see me.

"Change of plans Andrew. Please welcome to our home Mr. Stefan Pride. He will be my guest until he chooses otherwise." I told Andrew who I could see was apprising Stefan just as Stefan apprised him.

"Welcome Mr. Pride. Let me know of anything...anything at all that I can do to make your stay pleasant. For however long that may be." Andrew added.

"Andrew please have some wine and canapés sent to my office. We will be there shortly after I show Mr. Pride around a bit. Then please do not disturb us under any circumstances as we speak in private." I told him at the same time patting him on his back. He was gone in a flash to carry out my wishes.

"Should I even ask?" Stefan asked.

"You may if you want. But the answer will probably surprise you." I answered and then began to explain before Stefan could say anything to me. "Andrew has lived with me since he was a mere boy of fifteen. I had gone to one of the seedier parts of Boston to feed late one night. After having taken a minor amount of blood from a handsome young policeman who was walking his patrol and then sending him on his way, I heard glass breaking down a dark alley. Since that is where I had parked my car I hurried to investigate only to find Andrew trying to steal my favorite Maserati. I was infuriated! What was to have been a nice little outing was being ruined by this skinny little hoodlum. How many other lives had he upset with his acts of stealing? Angered, I covered the fifty feet from him to me in less than a second. He had no idea how or where I had even come from. My earlier feeding had been scant as is my way these days, but my anger fueled my need and I gripped the hapless youth to me like a rag doll and sank my fangs into his pulsing neck. Mine was the last car he would vandalize and attempt to steal.

"As his blood flowed into my mouth and down my throat I began to know him as I do all my 'food'. I saw the filthy little apartment crawling with roaches. I saw his crack dependent mother being fucked by a filthy dock worker and another huge bellied miscreant waiting his turn while my victim, but a small boy at the time watched helplessly. I felt the beatings from belts and fists bruising his body as they were dealt him by strange men. I could feel the fear he felt when men would lay money or meth on his mother's table before walking into the boy's room to do unthinkable things to him. It dawned on me that the world was little changed since I was his age.

"I stopped the flow of his blood. He was now unconscious, but I picked him up kissed his forehead, placed him in my car and brought him home with me. I nursed him back to health. I had the joy of watching him physically and mentally heal. With the help of a vampire friend of mine, whom you may later meet, we taught him to be a man and not to fear who he is or what had been done to him. We schooled him and we created documents for him. He was an incredibly quick read. What a brilliant mind he has and what a future. I will admit that I did wipe some of his memories because I felt then and still do that he need not be burdened with some of his past. But I want to make one thing clear. I never made him stay and when he was of age just four years ago he knew he was free to leave. He chose not to and for that I am grateful. While I may not be his father, I and my friend are as close to one as he has ever known and we are proud to be his friend.

He is actually in your university. He is just starting his first year of law school. Someday I wager that he will handle many of my affairs but at the same time I think he will devote his profession to assisting youths who even now live as he once did. He works for me here and wherever I happen to be living. Normally, he stays in my Boston penthouse due to the nearness of his university. But he thought I was taking you there and decided to come here and spend time with the lads that work here."

"I'm impressed," Stefan said, having listened intently to all I had said. "How many such young men do you employ and are they all like Andrew?"

"By the gods. No!" I quickly answered. "Around the world at my homes there are probably a hundred such young men and probably another hundred that are not so young anymore. All have been taken in by me when they were young. Yes they are all gay much to my delight. I pay them well and they all know who I am. I have forged a trust with them and only once over the centuries was that trust been broken, much to my sadness. All I send to school, should they decide to go and all are free to leave at any time. Stefan you are so obvious. You are wondering if I am physical with these boys. Absolutely I am. But it is by their free choice without tricks by me. They are just as physical with each other if and when they choose to be. I restate I have had sex with all my employees. I guess there could be a hell of a class action suit against me. I'll have to talk to Andrew and make sure he is not planning one." I laughed as Stefan looked at me, mouth agape. "Yes, I've had fun with all of them from the beginning with the exception of Andrew. He was my special one. Very fragile. I knew that he was like the others and me regarding sexual orientation but my orders were to leave him alone and let him come out in his own time. That he did. He has been with Todd, who is a tender thoughtful boy. Considering my feelings for him, I have never approached him. If he ever approaches me for the love that only two men can share I will probably do it. In fact I would probably be willing to gift him. That is how much I love him."

During this conversation we had walked out onto the veranda and now I had led Stefan back into the main house and up the stairs to my office library where a chilled wine bottle was set next to an assortment of canapés. I poured us each a glass and pointed to a seat. Once Stefan was seated I sat opposite him.

"So let's get this over with Stefan. I want you in my employ, not just because I enjoy looking at you. Now don't blush. You know most people do like to look at you. I want you because every sense I have says you can tell my story. In return you will get your degree and you will see the world both as we travel it and through my eyes. You will be privy to a life that is among the oldest on this planet. In return I expect complete trust and confidence. So ask away my young doubter." I prodded him. He took a sip of his wine and cleared his throat.

"Let me say sir that your offer is generous. Actually it is generous beyond my wildest dreams. I am also impressed by the story you told me of Andrew and, if true, your other boy...er...employees. Surely, though, you can imagine my skepticism. You are representing to me that you are a true vampire. That goes against everything I have been taught or believe." Stefan advised.

"Your point has been noted. How do you want me to prove it?" I asked.

"God, I don't know. Do something not human I guess. Show me your fangs."

I smiled at Stefan. He jerked back into the high back chair in which he was seated as two gleaming razor sharp incisors descended faster than he could see appear.

"Done." I stated simply. "What else?"

"Disappear into vapor." He ordered.

I made his mind see me turn to a blue white mist before his eyes and then vanish. He could no longer see me even though I was exactly where I was before. "Really Stefan this is quite tedious. How much longer must we do this?" My disembodied voice asked.

"Tell me something you should have no way of knowing about me."

"Fine," I said as I probed his mind now having reappeared to him. "What about you and Jack, your high school buddy. You were friends all through school. The last two years of high school all Jack could talk about were girls and sex. You always went along with his fantasies until that spring break of your senior year when the two of you convinced both your parents to let you go on a camping fishing trip. Jack saw it as a chance to drink beer and fish, but you were going to tell him your feelings." Stefan shifted uncomfortably in his chair. Before he could protest I started again. "That first day was great you both caught more than your share of fish. They smelled great cooking over the fire. You talked about how great it was to be graduating and getting the hell out of that town. You reminisced about childhood friends. As you got well into the case of beer you were able to buy with your fake ID the talk turned to pussy. Who put out and who didn't. Jack was noticeably rubbing across his crotch while he was talking. It was amazing how big his package was looking. You were hard too and you couldn't keep your eyes from where your friend was rubbing on himself. Jack was the first to bring out into the open how horny you both were eyeing his own crotch and then yours. You laughed nervously agreeing that you both were in a bad way. "What do you say we take care of it? There's no one around for miles. Let's just jerk off and get some fuckin relief man." I quoted Stefan's friend to him...sounding just like his buddy. "You hesitated and Jack said he was going to do it with or without you joining in. You often think of your best friend raising his ass up and unbuttoning his shorts before sliding them down his hips bringing that wild untrimmed bush into sight. You could see the thick root of his cock but the rest of it was pushed out of sight by his hand as he lowered his shorts more. Suddenly his cock escaped the bondage of his hand and sprung up, smacked the boy's belly and rose up pointing directly to Jack's navel.

You had seen Jack naked many times but never like this. His dick was even bigger than yours and that my dear boy is saying something. He looked at you and smiled as he locked his right hand as far around his staff as his fingers would reach just below that huge cap and he began to pump. Mesmerized for only a few seconds you pushed your shorts down to your knees and began stroking yourself slowly as you still watched semen leaking from Jack's dick as he continued to massage it. "Hey Stefan why don't you give me a hand with this? I know you want to and I've known for a long time. The truth is I want you to do it. What d'ya say, man. No one will know and we're going separate ways to school at the end of summer." Jack pleaded to you.

So Stefan, Jack was the first person to out you and being no fool you did not deny yourself. You reached over and pulled his hand off his cock and replaced it with your own and you began to pump slowly with your thumb pointed up just below the cap. That way you were able to catch the precum and use it as a lubricant to massage the thousands of nerve endings in his ridge. Without even thinking you found yourself laying between his hairy young thighs and licking those very ample balls as you continued your stroking. Jack was more surprised than you by the turn of events. In the back of Stefan Pride's mind was that if opportunity presents itself to do something you've dreamed of doing since you first discovered an attraction, best go for it. The next surprise for Jack was when you stopped licking his balls and starting sucking his cock. Your tongue twirled around the head as your bobbing head did a suction number. You truly blew that young man's mind. His excitement was such that he didn't last long and suddenly his gasping turned to moans as his balls contracted and the spasms of his cock worked his young thick sperm up that great tube of flesh. Jack tried to pull your head off and warn you that he was going to shoot but you held on and savored every last drop. When he had stopped writhing you took your mouth off him, then as an afterthought swiped out your tongue across the tip for one last oozing drop. Jack was laying there with his mouth open looking at you. You didn't say anything just lay there looking at your long time straight friend waiting for the shit to hit. "Stefan, that was the most incredible thing I have ever felt. Where did you learn that?" was all he could say. "Read about it." Was your simple response. "Well buddy you have good retention is all I can say. You can do that about any time you want unless I have a date lined up. But man for

your own sake we've got to always keep this between us."
You were lucky to have such a good friend. He left it up to
you to decide when and if you would ever come out in the
open. I see that you saw him during break and once again
took care of his needs. He's married now isn't he?" I asked
Stefan.

"Ok. Enough already!" Stefan said in an irritated fashion as
he swigged the last of his wine.

"Are you satisfied now Stefan? Or must we continue with
this 'prove I'm a vampire fiasco'? My time is valuable." I
stated in very gay feign of boredom.

"I'm not real sure how you knew about that or how you
sounded like Jack, but asking me to believe you are a true
vampire is still asking a lot. Show me if you're as fast as a
vampire is reputed to be. If you are, I will accept the job."
Stefan said, refilling his glass of wine.

"What the fuck just happened? What's going on?
Somebody help me!" screamed a frantic Stefan Pride.
Stefan, who had just been refilling his glass with some red
wine found himself in an altogether new situation. Not only
was the young journalist lying on the ancient Persian carpet
in my office, but he was stark naked. Further confusing the
situation was the fact his ankles were over my shoulders and
my cock was in his ass. Of course I was naked also.
Despite Stefan's anger and confusion about this
development in our interview I couldn't help but notice an
appreciative glance at my well defined chest and abdominal
area. He also looked with interest at my black curly pubic

hair and he no doubt could feel his heavy balls being supported by my cock which was a good six inches in his ass. I don't think however that he was as aware as I that he was lightly sweeping his hands back and forth across the breadth of my hairy thighs.

"Fast enough for you Mr. Pride?" I asked him.

"How dare you..." he started to protest before I interrupted him.

"Stefan, you have been thinking about this off and on since we met. I haven't done anything you did not want to do and it should have answered your final question." I told him matter of factly as I pushed in and out of him as we talked. I was hitting his young prostate dead on with each move and getting some groans of what I knew to be pleasure. "But I will pull out now and offer my most profound apologies and have you driven back to town if you so desire."

"Well, now that you've started you might as well finish." The boy said as he pushed himself to take more of me in his tight canal. Finish we did. I fucked this young stud long and hard. After ten minutes of nonstop deep and penetrating movement Stefan came without ever having touched himself. The eruption of sperm shot straight and true and I managed to catch the bulk of it in mid flight, savoring its spicy taste. When I had pulled out, Stefan was still shuddering from the orgasm. I lay him on his side, lowered myself on the carpet next to him, hoisted up his leg and slid my cock back in him. I slowly, at first fucked him, with long deep strokes and after a time picked up my pace. I had yet to come so my thrust became more rapid and finally vampire fast. As I exploded in this talented boy's ass he shot yet another copious load. I caught it in my cupped hand, which I brought to my lips and delighted in its taste once more. With some still in my mouth I turned his head toward me and with my dick still throbbing in his cute little butt I kissed him with my tongue going deep into his mouth thereby sharing with him his essence.

"When do I start Harry?" Stefan asked as we lay in the afterglow.

"Just as soon as you can make arrangements to move in to your quarters here, we will begin." I responded, as I pulled my staff out of his moist tightness with a wet pop. I reached down offering him a hand and a pull up from the floor. We stood facing each other briefly still admiring each other's body.

"Oh my God! Where did he come from?" Stefan yelled, as he tried in vain to cover his endowment with his hands. It seems Andrew had been just outside my office when he heard what he thought was a double culmination of pleasure. Being a very thoughtful young man he had taken it upon himself to bring a towel and a robe for Stefan.

Laughing, Andrew walked toward Stefan. I definitely caught a look of approval in my young ward's eye as he perused Stefan's much defined body with its well shaped generous appendage. "I just wanted to bring you a damp cloth to kind of clean up before you shower. It's not from firsthand knowledge yet but from past experience I know that sex with Mr. Alexander can be kind of messy." Alexander told the reddening boy as he pointed to a line of sperm running down the inside of Stefan's leg toward the carpet. "I also brought you a robe and towel. I'll get your clothes and lead you to your quarters where you can shower."

I wondered if my Andrew had an agenda of his own with my new assistant. Well, that was their business as long as it didn't interfere with his work or his schooling, I really didn't care.

So began the employment of Stefan Pride as my ghostwriter. Now let me get on with my story.

Chapter Two
About Vampires

There are a few more things you should understand about being a vampire. There are so many myths that have evolved over the ages. I wish to dispel you of a few, while others... well, let us just say I want to maintain some mystique so you shall remain unenlightened. The one myth that really mortifies me is the no reflection in the mirror thing. I assure you that I look at myself in the mirror at every opportunity because my looks keep me from any semblance of depression. The same holds true that a camera cannot capture our reflection. Rubbish! While I know some vampires who would be better off if this were true, I have been photographed all over the world in one of my careers as a model. The coffin idea blows too. In times gone by a sarcophagus was the ideal hiding place when we felt the need to withdraw and reflect. The sun, however, will not destroy us, give us a good tan, yes, but cancer or burn us......absurd. I have worshipped the sun gods of various cultures with the best of them. Furthermore, truth be told, I never sleep. I cannot turn into a bat, but I can make you think I do. A wooden stake through my heart will serve to really piss me off. I can fly, but it plays havoc with any fashion statements I may be demonstrating. The one truth is we must have blood.

Human blood is definitely the preference of every vamp I have ever known. But like everything else there is probably an exception somewhere in this world. Blood of any type will sustain us. Humans, any mammals, reptiles, or fish would maintain us. So you see like cockroaches we can get through the worst of times.

Certainly human blood will keep me in better humor and looking simply fabulous, so that is what I dine on. I do not have to kill my donor although at times I have killed. One of the many pluses of being over two thousand years old is my metabolism is refined to the point that very little fresh blood will sustain me for months, while a full meal can energize me for years. I have a theory that if I survive long enough I may not have to feed at all. Now that's a dreary prospect.

I can also make other vampires. It is rare that I or any of my brethren do that, however. It is time consuming to train a fledgling and usually we don't want the company. Certainly I have done it. But I am very particular with whom I share this gift. Many of you simply cannot handle it. Over the millennia I have created several children and with no small pride I will say that my choices have been exemplary. I and my "children" have benefited mankind to such an extent that humankind could not possibly repay its debt to us. That is why I was chosen to have immortality. But you will have to be the judge of that as I recount to you my centuries.

Upon my reawakening to my vampire existence I found that my mental acuity was a thousand times greater than in life. The various languages of man come to me as though through osmosis. By looking into the mind I could fathom every man's most minute and intimate thought. I had always been quite brilliant but I found I was now magnificent! Oddly enough, when I drink blood every memory of that person's life is revealed to me. So in a way, that individual's essence lives on long after they grow old and die. My healing abilities are almost instantaneous, my energy almost out of control at times and my strength formidable. I love battle and have fought in every major war, in which I believed, for the last twenty five hundred years.

In war I become one of you again. The smell from the sweat of my human comrades, the fear, and the testosterone assails me like an aphrodisiac. So you see, I am not all glamour, unless I want to be. Can I be destroyed? Yes. How? Let me just say there are ways, but share them with a small-minded world? I think not!

Chapter Three
My Early Life

I was born in the ancient land north of the city state of Athens in 356 BC in an area known as Macedon. I was the first and only surviving son of a Macedonian aristocrat named Amyntor, a naturalized Macedonian citizen, originally from Athens. Our estate was in the city of Miezo. Our land was ruled by King Phillip II. I had a normal and happy childhood. My father doted on me, his only heir. From the earliest time I can remember I was always at his side. He never missed taking me to the city square so that I might witness the execution of those who had breached some law (whether the law was written yet or not) or to the practice fields to watch the king's brave soldiers send enemy captives to be with the gods. Those were truly good times. You might think this barbaric. Not so! It is happening in your world even as you read of my life.

I was schooled in every modern mode of warfare and I excelled! There are some detractors who think I did not, but I disagree. Certainly I will not go so far as to say that I was the best of my time, that title can only be claimed by one other, but I was good and my strategies beyond reproach. At the age of thirteen I was privileged to become a royal page, a role common to adolescent boys of the aristocratic class in my country. It was at this time in the king's palace that I met the boy who would become the only person I have ever completely loved. His name was Alexander IV. As I told you my name was Hephaestion (still is but now I go by Harry Alexander. Imagine the butchery of telemarketers calling for Hephaestion... let's not even go there). Anyway, there were about fourteen noble youths in this academy.

Our teacher was none other than Aristotle, the great philosopher. One might think Aristotle agreed to teach us because he saw in us potential scholars who would pass on his knowledge to future generations. But alas, the truth is, king Phillip promised to rebuild Aristotle's hometown, which the king had leveled, and to free all the townsmen, now enslaved, if Aristotle would take on our education. So it was agreed. The academy was in the temple ruins of some god no longer in favor with the king.

Now, let us get back to Alexander. I don't know if it was love or lust at first sight but certainly an unshakeable friendship formed. In rapid time, I came to love him and he me. Olympias, Alexander's mother, did not care for me. She felt I was a bad influence on her son because while he showed no interest in females, word was all over the palace regarding our rutting activity. But she tolerated me and eventually would become a confidante. In fact she preferred me by far to any of the women that were destined to share her son's bed.

By the time we were a few years into our teens I was his erastes and he my eromenos. History has that the other way around. In truth I was his lover and he was my beloved. In our few years to be together we were alter egos. Some historians have written that we were one soul with two bodies. For me there was no other love but Alexander. I would have gone to the end of the world for him. Actually, I did.

He had visions of ruling the entire known world and out of

my love for him I made his vision my vision and I gave the world to him. He would probably tell this story differently but he isn't the one telling it, is he? I can honestly say that I fell in love with the man's soul (there are some who would argue that his nine inch cock didn't hurt his appeal either) and not his looks, which were quite pleasing to me. For a Macedonian he was somewhat short but he had an angelically beautiful face, luscious firm lips, almost feminine eyes, and thick dark blond hair, quite unusual for our race. He was always cleanly shaven even though his beard was heavy and darker than the rest of his body hair. His pecs were chiseled with a light dusting of hair. His cock was beautiful befitting his royal station. It was fairly thick and long growing from a curly bush of very dark blond hair. His only flaw was a slight congenital defect...a twist to his neck or something. It has been immortalized by some sculptors of the day. I believe today it is called scoliosis. But he was so physically beautiful and his persona so awe inspiring, that this did not detract from him. Rather it added to his look, giving him the appearance of looking up to the heavens and his head slightly cocked as if hearing advice from the gods. It was really only noticeable to me when I would trace his spinal cord with my fingers as he lay on top of me while he pistoned his cock in and out of my wanting asshole.

Because I had shared Alexander's upbringing I had, early on, learned to fight and to ride as well as he. My first taste of military action was the campaign against the Thracians while Alex was regent. Soon after this I participated in King Phillip's Danube campaign in 342BC and only four years later in the battle of Chaeronea, while I was still a mere teenager. Historically you will not be able to find my name mentioned among the lists of high-ranking officers during these early battles of Alexander's Danube campaign or even the invasion of Persia. The reason for that is a simple one. I coexisted with Alexander to the extent that if he was on a campaign it can be assumed that I was at his side. Most times when my name is mentioned by historians it is regarding some occurrence that took place when we were not together. Also, my promotions were achieved through merit and not my ability to milk Alexander's cock!

Early on, however, I was privileged to be appointed as a member of Alexander's personal bodyguard, the Somatopphylakes. This elite group consisted of seven men, drawn from the Macedonian nobility, who also acted as high-ranking military officers. Understand, this was not a group of body guards but an assembly of men who fought at his side in battle. Thus, I was given the title of Chiliarch; today the closest translation would be general.

Now that I have brought up the subject of Alexander's cock, I also need to mention that he truly was the best lover I have had to date and that is saying something. We could and did spend hours just sucking each other's cock. Our kisses made us forget whose tongue was whose and when he fucked me I could hear the Sirens of Homer's saga sing. I am getting too poetic, aren't I? So if you don't like it put the book down. Sometimes we would fuck so long and hard that in a state of exhaustion we would sleep with his cock still buried deeply within me. I swear upon my immortality that Alexander was the only man to enter me during the course of my entire life time; such was my devotion to him.

I will not go so far as to say that he was my one and only during my life. I am, after all, no fool. I had not only thousands of soldiers that would do anything to taste or feel my cock and slaves by the hundred score to do my bidding even if they were not of my persuasion. But I tended to be discrete. On the other hand, Alexander viewed sex and love differently than I. I mean that even after two thousand years of constantly reflecting on our relationship, I am confident that he "loved" only me. Never-the-less, he fucked and sucked every soldier and eunuch he could get it up for.

Alexander looked beyond the sex of a person. He did not see race or ethnicity, rather he saw beauty. It was beauty that fired his lust more than gender. Believe me it was more than once I made issue of this. He used the argument that men of this century still use (and which still doesn't work for me) that "it was only sex". Upon his death I would often think of his infidelities. I found such thoughts a useful tool that helped to ease the pain of my grief. Again, I have wandered off track.

You also need to know that my short career was not just a military one. From the beginning I was engaged in special missions, sometimes diplomatic, often technical. Whereas, Alexander was quick to anger and saw little advantage to reasoning with the enemy, I had the ability to reason with people and the patience to get what we wanted. One instance that comes to mind is a diplomatic mission after the battle of Issus when my man, Alexander, was going south down the Phoenician coast and had received the capitulation of Sidon, I was authorized to appoint to the throne the

Sidonian I considered most deserving of that office and one who would have allegiance to Alexander. After asking around I found and chose a man distantly related to the royal family whose good morality had reduced him to working as a gardener. I still remember him well. His name was Abdalonymus and he had a popular and successful royal career. He remained regent long after Alexander and I were gone. Thus it was that my choices were well thought and became even more respected as time progressed.

Chapter Four
Aristenes

Another instance of my success that I can bring to your attention happened after the siege of Tyre in 332BC when I was at the young age of twenty-four. Alexander had entrusted his fleet to me with orders to skirt the coast and head for Tyre, our next objective, while my Alexander led the army overland.

Alexander could really pick my tasks and this was not an easy one. Because you see, this was not the Athenian fleet with which Alexander had started. He had disbanded that one and I found myself in charge of a collection of semi-reluctant men of many nationalities who I had to hold together through great patience and my personal character strength. After I finally got to the ruins of old Tyre I realized that the siege engines would have to be unloaded, transported across hellish terrain, and then reassembled. Of course it was achieved largely through my ability to command and my uncanny choice of the right sailors to fuck. The latter is why so many of these ragtag studs were so loyal to me as to enlist in Alexander's army and follow his caravan for years to come.

As I had mentioned earlier, my navy and its men were not of just one common country, but were quite diverse in its makeup. However, among the men manning our ships were some who shared my own culture. One such sailor was Aristenes, a fellow countryman. He had become a member of this temporary fleet through no doing of his own. At the age of fourteen Aristenes had been orphaned as a result of a piracy raid on his seaside village along the ancient Grecian coast. What modest wealth his family had was gone and there were no agencies in those times to provide for him. Being a big strong lad he had managed to work and travel on merchant ships. By the time I had befriended him he was a well-seasoned merchant sailor of eighteen.

I had spotted Aristenes the first day I sailed Alexander's fleet toward Tyre. I made inquiries about him and learned that he was of Macedonian descent. He had no rank, but being one of my own countrymen would make speaking with him a pleasure. I also learned that he had picked up a number of languages from his travels as a merchant seaman. For a young man, whose education had been cut short, he definitely had a gift for learning. Being multi-lingual and intelligent would make him invaluable to me. It came to me that I could benefit by becoming his sponsor…in many ways.

While certainly not a slave, Aristenes had no rank in this haphazard fleet. I was attracted to him the first day of our sail not only from what I had learned about him but because of the grace he possessed and his beauty. His voice was a rich baritone, unusual for one so young and he addressed both his equals and the slaves with respect. I could tell by watching him that he also had the respect of the galley men with whom he labored. Furthermore, he carried himself with the posture and dignity of an educated aristocrat.

It was under these circumstances that I had him brought before me in my small cabin. If he was nervous in my presence he did not show it. On the other hand he did not act overly confident either. No doubt he knew more about me than I about him. He was likely aware that he was standing before the second most powerful person in the world. He was a smart lad. I was direct and to the point with him.

"Aristenes you will be my assistant and my tongue to these men. What say you?" I asked.

His eyes properly lowered, not in fear but in the respect due me, he replied. "That would give me undeserved honor

Chiliarch. I will do all I can to prove myself worthy of your judgment."

"Very well then, get back to your present duties. Later I will give you your new assignments and make it clear to your senior officer just what they are."

"Yes Chiliarch". With that Aristenes did a sort of about face and started for the door of my cabin.

"One more thing Aristenes." I said stopping him in his tracks. Turning around he faced me questioningly. "Sir?" he asked. His eyes once more dropping in another show of respect.

"You will be sleeping with me tonight and every night until I inform you otherwise." I said casually to the youth.

"At your request Chiliarch. Is there anything else?" the boy asked without emotion.

"No, just make sure you are bathed and clean outside...and in," I told him as an afterthought. "Among your regular duties will be to provide me relief when I need it. For the time being I am the only man whose cock you will service. Clear?" I asked him.

"As you wish Chiliarch." He paused and then like the man he was put a question to me. "Would it be forward of me to tell you that I will do as you desire with great happiness?" The boy spoke the question softly. Did I note a slight color rise in his face?

I am sure that a smile betrayed my firmness. "You may", I told him. With that Aristenes was out the door and about his chores.

That, my dear readers, was the beginning of a long and true friendship. Aristenes, while receiving no promotions, would share my bed frequently when I was not with my beloved Alexander. Because his comrades thought he was in my bed only to keep my cock milked for me, a job any of them upon my order might have had, he appeared to receive no real favoritism from me. This meant that he would be privy to their thoughts and conversations. His loyalty to me was such that he confided all to me and I was able to carefully craft my authority over my men. I have little doubt that it was the help of my little Aristenes that made my movement of men and equipment to Tyre the success that it was destined to be.

I can remember that first night on the ship with Aristenes as if it were an hour ago. The sea was smooth as glass. There was no moon but the stars were so bright that the torches were not really needed for seeing. The men had labored well and hard that day and the ship had quieted early as sleep overcame them. I was at my table drawing some last minute plans for our landing in a couple of days when there was a light knock on my cabin door. "Enter!" I said in my most authoritative tone. The door opened and without hesitation in stepped Aristenes. What a beautiful youth he was. His skin was quite light for a Greek and he had masses of dark luxuriant curls that fell to his shoulders. Like most of my countrymen, his eyes were brown but his were to the point of being black and would have been except for some golden flecks that would favor you when the light angled on them in just the right way. His eyelashes were long and so thick they appeared double in growth. The lips were full and red. The face had not yet a hint of beard corrupting it. I could smell that he was indeed clean as he stood before me with his eyes cast to the ground and his arms hanging demurely at his sides. His garment was short and was held up by one strap over his shoulder coming up from the linen girdle around his slim waist. He was wearing the leather sandals that laced up around his smooth muscular shins to his knees in the fashion of a merchant marine.

"Aristenes," I quietly said to him.

"My lord. "He responded.

"Lift up your head and look into my eyes," I commanded him. Slowly and shyly he did as told. "I want you to listen and listen to me well. When you are in my presence and it is just the two of us, I want you to hold your head up and look me in my eyes when we speak to each other. You are not my slave you are a fellow countryman who I would very much like to have as a friend. Do I make myself clear?"

"As my lord commands," was his reply with no little surprise showing in his eyes.

"Very well then, the hour grows late and I grow weary and need to go to sleep. Disrobe my young sailor. Your commander has a cock in great need of relief!" I bid him as if I were many more than just six years his senior.

Aristenes immediately loosened his tunic and undid the girdle, which fell to the floor. His body was a sight to behold. The muscles in his legs looked to be chiseled from marble. His abdomen taunt from his hard work glistened with an oil he had applied after his bath. His cock was glorious even in its relaxed state. Its root sprung from a forest of glossy black curls and its shaft extended over his large low hanging balls, which were encased in a smooth satiny looking sac. The tip of his foreskin was not overly pronounced but clearly indicated an impressive head beneath its cloak of skin.

"You are as beautiful and more then I would have ever surmised," I said to him as I undid my robe and quickly followed suit with my loin cloth.

I now stood before the youth naked. My cock not yet hard but I could feel the twitching of expectation. I walked the few steps to my cot picked up a bottle of precious oil and handed it to the boy. I could tell there was some confusion in his eyes and then it dawned on me. This boy had no idea what to do or what was expected of him exactly. I was going to have to train him! Just my luck to get an inexperienced youth! You have no idea what a delight that revelation was for me. This had not happened to me since Alexander and I had mutually learned how to pleasure each other around the time hair had started to sprout around our young cocks. This was a fantastic way to start a war campaign on Tyre!

"I appreciate that you are not familiar with the ways of warriors but not to worry. This is not a concern sailor. This is very light aromatic oil. It is used in the courts of Persia as both a skin rejuvenator and also as a source of pleasure. I am going to lie down and I want you to pour small amounts into your hands and by rubbing apply it to my skin. Start at my feet and rub the oil into my body from foot to head." The boy was a quick read and in just a few minutes had worked his way to my muscular thighs, running his fingers through the curly hair on my legs which tickled erotically. By this time my dick was at full attention with its head beginning to peek out of the tip of my foreskin and stretching to my navel, as it throbbed in conjunction with my heartbeat. Aristenes, I could tell, was having trouble keeping his eyes off my pride.

"Do not rub the oil on my staff. We will do that later. Continue to massage my chest and arms just as you have been doing." And so he did. When this was complete I flipped over on my stomach and without instruction the boy started massaging my feet once more and working his way up the back of my fuzzy legs. There was some hesitation when he reached the smooth cheeks of my ass.

"Why have you stopped boy?" I asked. Not a little disgruntled at being brought out of my relaxed state.

"Chiliarch, I have never touched a man here before and I stopped not wanting to offend you," was his only reply.

Laughing at his timidity, I assured him, "Trust me I will not be offended. Massage each side well and continue up my back." And so he proceeded, carefully avoiding that sensitive entrance to my body. I smiled to myself knowing what a delight it was going to be when I taught him another use of a man's most private spot.

All of this massaging had taken probably an hour perhaps a little longer. My young man was showing no signs of fatigue, but I knew that he had labored hard in the hot sun all that day and surely must be exhausted. I decided that in fairness to him that I would speed this night's activity up and go lightly on him the next day.

"All right sailor have you ever had a man's cock in your mouth?" I asked him as I turned over on my back and looked at him as he sat on his knees at the side of my cot.

Nervously Aristenes eyed my engorged penis and then looked at me. "No Chiliarch. I have seen many of the men on ships do that before sleeping, but usually they pleasure themselves. Some even offered to stick their cocks into my mouth but somehow it never came about. I have had my staff in the mouth of several men and some women as well for my payment of food and a place to sleep before I became a merchant's sailor." The young man answered me with what I knew to be truth in his tone. Oh this was going to be fun. I knew then that this youth's sailor days of being a merchant sailor were at an end!

"Very well Aristenes. This time fate will not interfere and it is going to come about. I want you to hold the base of my cock like so," I instructed him by taking his right hand and wrapping it around the base of my cock. His thumb and index finger were unable to touch such was my girth. "Now bring your lips to the tip of my staff and lave it with your tongue." Aristenes followed my request without a question. "Now open your mouth and careful not to hit it with your teeth take as much of me as you can into your throat. Ahh yes that's it! As you pull back on it apply some suction and when you near the tip do the same thing again. So do it just as those men and women did to you." I instructed him softly while my hand worked its way through the thick curls on his head. He did as told and he applied just enough pressure on his second downward stroke to peel back my foreskin with his lips. His tongue went to work licking that sensitive part at the underside of the cap. In no time he had my precum flowing and was eagerly swallowing it. His gag reflex was there but each time he quickly overcame it and was milking my cock with gusto. This went on for probably ten minutes and not having been with Alexander for at least a week I was on the verge of shooting my thick white essence down his throat.

Pushing his head back and hearing that plop as my cock

was released from his mouth I had exited just in time to avoid climaxing. Aristenes looked at me as if he had done something wrong. "Stop with the worried look. You were more then I would have dared hope for on this trying voyage. I need to sleep as do you." He looked somewhat crestfallen at this. So taking pity on him I said, "But in consideration of our situation and the possibility that one or both of us may die for the glory of my beloved Alexander, it would be remiss of me not to instruct you in the Greek art of pleasing a man."

My sailor smiled. "I am your willing student Chiliarch. What should I learn that I may please you more?" The young sailor asked with plump red lips that yet glistened with my semen still on them. With that question asked so eagerly, the training of Aristenes in the art of warrior love began.

"Had your father not perished at the hands of the pirates who raided your village, he would have reached an agreement with an older learned man to lecture and teach you Greek thought. Certainly, this man would have been considerably older than me, but I am sure enough of my knowledge to take on the role of mentor." I told him with confidence. The fact was, while his father would have indeed contracted with a learned citizen, the man chosen to school Aristenes would certainly have been older than me by many years. I was at best of an age to be his older brother. But these were uncertain times and someone had to take on the responsibility of training this youth in all that was Greek! Who better than me? Later as I got to know Aristenes better I realized what a load of bullshit this probably sounded like to him. But he handled the situation admirably.

"My Chiliarch I have been placed in your hands and at your

service for whatever you feel I can do that is in your best interest. If what you teach me is something my father would have condoned it is so much the better!" What a shame the youth of today do not walk in his footsteps.

"Very well, I want you to take the oil and generously apply it to my cock." This done I instructed him to get in an all fours position on my cot. Having taken the oil from him I drizzled some between his lovely firm cheeks as well as on my fingers. Slowly and with care I reached under him with my left hand and took hold of his large velvety cock and began a sensual stroke thereof. I heard the sigh from him. With my right hand well anointed I felt between his cheeks until I found the rosebud of his entrance. Using my index finger I slid across it lightly circling to a stop. At this point I began my insertion. I heard an audible gasp when my finger was all the way his tight sweet ass. After just a short while I withdrew my finger to the point where the tip was just clutched by his sphincter muscle. Then I added a second finger and finally a third. The boy was definitely grunting in pain but did not pull away. Rather he pushed back to take more of my fingers up his arse. After I had left them in his ass for what I felt to be an appropriate time I withdrew totally.

"Now Aristenes, I want you to keep your ass up but lay your head against the cot resting your head on your hands." The youth quickly complied. "Now I am going to replace my fingers with my cock. This is going to cause you considerable discomfort at first. In fact it will be a white fire like burn as you are stretched. But I am being considerate of you and going slowly at the cost of my own enjoyment in order that you might learn." I told him.

"Yes Chiliarch do what you will with me. AAGGhh!" He screamed into the cot padding as I thrust the large head of my cock into his hole and passed the tight muscle.

"Just relax. The burning will go away and I promise that you will beg for me to fuck you often and hard." I assured him.

From my position behind him I was able to see the side of his face and the look of pain. I also noted tears running down his cheek and onto the bed. But not once did he pull away. After a short while I could feel him relax and just as with my fingers he began to push back on my throbbing staff. I was in maybe four inches when I pulled back with just the head staying inside the muscle ring and then easing back in to five inches and so on until I was buried eight inches into his ass. My cock hair was flattened against his smooth cheeks and I could feel my balls touching his sac when I moved back into him.

The tightness and the heat were an incredible combination. Each time I pulled back his canal sucked on my dick, loathe to release it from its moist grip. I began my fucking in earnest, pounding his ass and reveling in the sound of his grunts which were now sounds of pleasure. I too was grunting as I thrust every inch into this boy I had met just this morning. As with all things it had to end and I blasted my seed into his gut for no less than ten spurts. As the pearly white seed shot into the youth I could feel the sperm as it made its way out of his hole, dripping onto my tight balls. I rested then with my staff remaining in him for an indeterminate time. Finally I pulled out with a wet sucking plop. He grunted from the feel of being suddenly empty of dick just as I had often done when Alexander would wean me from his monster. I remember thinking Alexander will like my milker.

I was exhausted but not yet ready to end this most enjoyable evening. I turned the boy over onto his back. His huge thick cock lay in a slight curl against his abdomen unspent and copiously leaking semen onto his smooth belly, which had not even a hint of treasure trail. Later when our fucking became more familiar and pleasurable to him, his cock would fire its essence without ever being touched. But how could I leave him like this when he had been so terribly cooperative with me?

"Now Aristenes, I am going to do something that no tutor would ever do." With those words I plunged my mouth down on his cock taking it to its fresh smelling hairy root and began earnestly blowing this young sailor. In less than a minute he made those sounds boys still make today letting me know he was going to come. Spurt after spurt came in my mouth. I was determined not to lose even a drop. True to my oral skill none of the precious liquor was lost.

While in ancient Greek culture it was quite acceptable for an older man, often a family friend, to take on a youth for training in the ways of citizenship, it was not acceptable for two male adults to have oral sex. This is something that while frequently practiced just wasn't talked about.

"I find the drinking of a young man's essence to be enjoyable and good for me. I emphasize it is something that you will never mention but something that will frequently happen. Understood?"

"Yes my Chiliarch!" And then we slept until sunrise.

Chapter Five
Taking the Island of Tyre

By the time we had arrived, the unloading of ships and supplies begun in a well organized rush. Equipment and men were unloaded and we sat about assembling our machines of destruction. Alexander did not like calling his equipment by this name. He preferred to label machines as liberation devices since were freeing the people of this land from their present form of government. Regardless of how you look at it, they were lethal inventions.

These siege machines were massive considering they were not equipped with wheels and would not be for several centuries. Alexander's father had been instrumental in the development and improvement of many of the war machines of which we made use. Some leaders foster and support social programs, Alexander and his father pioneered instruments of war.

For this battle I had the men work in shifts for several days assembling our catapult artillery. There were two main types we used. To make a grand entrance we had the lithobolos, which was a stone-thrower. It was a giant sling mounted on a heavy wooden frame. We also made use of a dart thrower. This beauty stood three to four feet high and shot huge arrows. The lithobolos did the more damage but the dart thrower was definitely the more accurate. I had also brought along spring powered artillery. One in particular was an engine we called katapeltai or sometimes just mechanai. It was another form of dart thrower that had an effective range of over three hundred meters.

A couple of days after we had arrived I received word of approaching ships. I feared the worse, thinking that Tyre was getting help. I knew my small force of soldiers and ill trained naval crew would not have a chance against seasoned naval warriors. My distress was laid to rest when I learned that we had new allies. It seemed the naval commanders of the Phoenician cities of Aradus and Byblus, impressed by Alexander's victory at Issus, abandoned the Persian admiral Autophradates, with whose fleet they had been serving, and deserted to Alexander. In addition, ten triremes (a very fast ship in those days deriving its name from its three rows of oars on each side, manned with one man per oar) also came over to us from Rhodes. Then a few hours later I learned that another thirteen such vessels joined us from the cities of the Lycian and Cilician coasts, and a fifty-oared galley came from Macedon itself. The massive desertion of the Phoenicians, with eighty ships, had its repercussions in Cyprus, whose kings were also anxious to be on the winning side. A combined Cyprian fleet of one hundred twenty ships soon sailed to us, swelling our growing navy as it lay in readiness.

Also helpful was the fact that Alexander had many weeks before sent Cleander, the son of Polemocrates, to Greece to recruit mercenaries and that dependable young man had returned with a body of four thousand Peloponnesian troops. The Tyreans now stood even less of a chance. Alexander, I knew, was going to be extremely pleased.

During the interval of my shaping up the navy and transporting our equipment Alexander had busied himself with a foray into Arabian territory inland, and after a ten-day demonstration of strength, in which he used a few cavalry squadrons, he received the submission of the people in this area. While he regarded the raids as a military training exercise, it fit well with his general strategy of leaving no active enemy in his rear.

The Tyre campaign was a wonderful event. Alexander was to meet me with his army the next day. But this day was hot and there was no breeze. I, like all of my soldiers, was sweaty, miserable, and irritable. I had successfully overseen the reassembly of our formidable siege machines and they would be used with purpose. The sun had been over the horizon but three hours when a scout came galloping into our encampment with word that Alexander was but an hour away. My beloved had made it to me a full day ahead of time.

"That is indeed wonderful news soldier. Quench both you and your horse's thirst with water and ride out to meet Alexander. Tell him that his servant Hephaestion awaits him with great joy at his safe and speedy journey."

"Yes my Chiliarch!"

"Prepare the king a bath and a dinner and set both up in the royal tent. We have much to discuss before tomorrow's battle and the king will need to be refreshed." I ordered an officer standing near me.

"My Chiliarch!" he responded. Immediately preparations began for the king's arrival.

A full half an hour before Alexander and his army could be seen, we were able to see vast plumes of dust in the air made by the movement of his approach. I was busy seeing that the tables were in place where we would lay out our battle strategy before our ranking commanders later that day as I knew Alexander would want. Calmly I moved about issuing orders that I knew would be obeyed to the letter and without question of purpose. Inside I was not so calm. I never was when I had been absent from Alexander for any length of time. I was starved for his attention and the feel of his lips on mine. I always was.

Still to this day I hunger for those lips. I will never feel their kiss again nor will I thrill to the ecstasy of fullness that I felt when he would enter me. I long for the words of love he would whisper to me. I wish to hear again the tender sounds and feel the subtle movements to which no other in our world was made privy. Only now, twenty-three centuries later do I divulge our intimacies. And to whom am I telling it? To a world and time empty of the fire of passion and dispossessed of original thought! We were definitely not the picture history has painted. My mind often screams into the void caused by his absence. It was an absence that I could have prevented. Pardon me once more dear mortal readers. I wander off subject again.

"Majesty it is a good surprise to see you here at this early time," I said to my king in the respectful tone due him before his men.

"Hephaestion it is also good to see you and know that you met target and are here prepared to bring our enemies to their knees!" replied the king as we approached each other, our arms out to grasp the shoulders of the other, as was custom. Then into the empty royal tent we walked.

"I took the liberty of having a bath prepared for you," I advised Alexander.

"By the gods Hephaestion cut the shit! Every time we are apart for more than a few days you treat me like you are my servant. I can assure you that it is no secret amongst our men that we milk each other and have since we were able to spurt," Alexander said to me with no little aggravation in his voice. This was a lecture that I had heard many times before. What can I say? I was just really into decorum.

"Alexander I know that. I just..." the sentence was never finished as Alexander crushed his lips against mine and forced his tongue between them. Automatically I wrapped my arms around him returning both the kiss and the probe of my tongue. One of Alexander's hands was held against the small of my back and the other had deftly slipped under my garment and was cupping my left ass cheek. Finally after what seemed like forever but was actually too soon, Alexander released me and stood back looking me up and down.

"Undress Hephaestion I have thought of little else for the past three hours other than you standing before me naked."

"Alexander I want that too. But you are filthy and sweaty from your journey and your bath waits. There are six generals just the other side of the tent flap waiting to hear your strategy, and Tyre is preparing to defend itself against us." I cautioned him.

"I am king! You think I am not aware of all you just told me?" he huffed in his most majestic tone. All the while a smile played on his succulent mouth.

"The bath can wait. I think it is important that you be reminded of the heady aroma of sweat in a man's pits and the musk of sweating balls. You have languished too long in the comfort of a ship. The generals can wait at the entrance to our tent while I am satiated. The people of Tyre can prepare a little longer before meeting their fate. Now undress and kneel before me little playmate." Thus spoke my king as he himself set about disrobing. I was somewhat offended that he thought of me languishing in luxury in that smelly leaky vessel, but thought better than to mention it.

Soon enough as he had bid I was on my knees before him with that great veined cock standing at attention before me. In anticipation of his pleasure there was already precum dripping over the tip of his thick foreskin. For myself, I was already salivating at the prospects of sucking this man in his natural state. I reached up with my right hand and taking hold of his love muscle I drew it down to mouth level. The aroma was erotic beyond my ability to describe it. (Just a note for future reader understanding, I am really into clean men, but with Alexander the intoxicating smell of sweat, seminal fluid, and piss that had fermented under his foreskin was fantastic.) Pushing back the encasement of skin I eagerly licked around my love's cockhead. His manhood was throbbing and sighs issued from Alexander's throat telling me that I was doing exactly what he wanted and needed. After many years of sucking a cock the size of Alexander's, my gag reflex was all but gone and I deep throated him as he shoved his dick repeatedly pass my lips, crushing my nose into his aromatic golden hairs. In due time, I pulled back and twirled my tongue around the head of his cock as I released it from my mouth. I then pressed my lips against his balls and began to lick them clean. Their scent was a mixture of his sweat, leather from his saddle and even the wafting up of horse sweat from his muscular hairy thighs. Being with this man in this way was one of the things that had made my life worth living and still fills my death with reason to remember.

At last I rose up from my knees, walked to the bed and lay on my back with my knees bent to my chest and parted. As a general rule Alexander liked to fuck me after being away from each other for a while.

"No Hephaestion. I am tired and stressed. I need you to fill me this time." With that, Alexander gripped my hand and pulled me up. He assumed my position lying on his back with his ankles on my shoulders. Bath oil was in a small glass vessel near the bed. I spread this liberally on my staff and massaged an ample amount in and around his asshole. With my left hand around the musculature of his right thigh and my right hand around the base of my cock I guided my manhood to the point of entry. Pushing slowing, I made little headway into his tightness.

"Hephaestion! You are not busting a virgin. You've been there before. You are a Chiliarch. Assault me!" Alexander commanded. Well my king only had to command. I thrust forward passed his muscle ring and eight inches deep in one push. Alexander screamed from the initial pain and grunted loudly from the next five full thrusts. The screams brought in four guards with sword in hand. The looks on their faces when they saw their young king laying on his back and his legs wrapped around the waist of his young best friend being skewered by that same friend's cock was priceless. In unison we were given the perfunctory bow and they quickly exited the tent.

"You did that on purpose, didn't you Hephaestion?" Alexander stated breathlessly recovering from pain somewhat.

"Majesty, I am not the one who screamed like a little girl. I only follow orders." I said innocently. He started to protest but I put my lips against his forcefully and began thrusting in earnest. For at least fifteen minutes we fucked and this time we were both making loud lust-filled sounds. No doubt there would be soldiers that night horny and fucking with thoughts of us in their fantasy.

I knew that my fucking was coming to an end as I felt the buildup of juice and its promise of orgasmic release. One long last thrust and I pumped out thick ribbons of sperm deep into his gut and with numerous little twitching jabs forward I kept spurting into him. At the same time I was doing this Alexander started spewing seed so thick that it was in clumps on his chest and it even hit our faces. I smiled down at him and bowing my head down to the nearest stream of spunk I lapped it off his chest and then shared it with him in a deep kiss. Looking into each other's eyes at the same instant we both whispered "I love you." Shortly afterwards servants were brought in and they cleaned both of us. The generals were assembled and our plans for Tyre were laid out.

The island of Tyre was a somewhat bloody battle. When the Tyrians recognized the superiority of the numbers against them they prudently avoided an open water conflict, concentrating instead on holding the entrance of their harbors in the face of the oncoming enemy; any fighting would then be in narrow waters, where Alexander's numbers could not be deployed to advantage.

The two harbors of the island faced north and south respectively, one towards Sidon, the other towards Egypt. Seeing their entrances heavily defended, Alexander did not at once try to force an entry. The mouth of the north harbor, as he approached, was blocked by battleships moored bow-on to him. But his Phoenician galleys sank three exposed position, ramming them head-on.

This went on for some days until the Tyrean navy was pretty much destroyed. Then the hard part of our conquest was yet to come. The walls of Tyre were now a somewhat formidable obstacle. In the north, the Greek contingent towed up siege engines, but the solidity of the walls defied their efforts. In the south, a part of the wall was slightly shaken, and small breach was made, into which gangways were tentatively thrown. But our own Macedonian assault using the gangways was being easily repulsed by the Tyrians.

After this brief encounter, we berthed our ships along the mainland shore and encamped on the adjacent land at a point where the hills gave some protection from the weather. Our own headquarters were southwards, looking towards the island's southern harbor. We ordered the Cyprian fleet to blockade the north side of the island and the Phoenicians the south.

We had meanwhile recruited a large number of artificers both from Cyprus and the Phoenician coast. The construction of siege engines had thankfully come along swiftly, no small thanks to Aristene's help, and these were installed on the extremity of the mole as well as on the besieging ships, both transports and slow battleships, which we had caused to be anchored all around the city preparatory to bombarding the high walls. (The walls were enormous at one hundred fifty feet high on the side facing the mole.) The masonry opposite the mole was massive, consisting of large mortared stone blocks. On top of these, the Tyrians had built wooden towers in order that they might increase their advantage of height, and they showered down missiles of every kind, including the fire-darts, on our besieging ships. As a further device, they piled rocks in the sea under their walls, and this kept our vessels at a distance. We hauled away the rocks, as far as possible but this work had to be carried on from ships anchored nearby, and it was a slow process.

After some three days and weather favoring us we were able to have more of our siege engines towed up to the area where we had made the most headway and with our combined efforts we were able to widen the breach. Still this was not enough as week after week we fought to claim this city. But with time and by making widespread diversions all around the perimeter of the city, the besieging ships managed to move close under the walls. At last we were achieving the desired effect. The sector of the wall where Alexander himself was taking part in the assault was the first to be captured. Some of the towers that were atop the battlements were now occupied by our forces. Soon our men were fighting their way down into the city itself.

I almost lost Alexander to an arrow which missed his heart by three inches. Fortunately it was a shoulder wound that would heal in time. This siege had taken seven months to complete. As punishment, both for resisting us and injuring the king, all men, just as in the defeat of some other conquests, were put to death by sword and the women and the children were sold into slavery. This battle and the taking of Gaza (a land battle) soon after, lowered all resistance in the area. Jerusalem opened its gates to us. Egypt looked at us as liberators.

Chapter Six
A Surprise for the New Pharaoh

Egypt was an exotic and strange land. It was a land full of mystery and more ancient than we could fathom. Alexander was named pharaoh and son of the god Amun at the oracle of Siwas Oasis in the Libyan dessert. After that he often referred to Zeus-Ammon as his true father, and subsequent currency depicted him with ram horns as a symbol of his divinity, which he ate up. During our stay in Egypt, we founded Alexandria-by-Egypt, which was to become the prosperous capital of the Ptolemaic Kingdom some years down the road.

I should also mention that it was in Egypt that I decided to surprise Alexander with a prized possession that I had considered keeping just for myself. It was after a long day of endless meetings with our officers and technicians concerning how best to proceed in completing our destruction of Darius; making all that he had once ruled a part of our empire. Having retired to our suite for a quiet dinner and further discussion on what our think tank had proposed, I told Alexander I had a surprise for him but that it would have to wait for after dinner.

"Hephaestion you know I hate it when you try to be mysterious." He pouted. "Don't tell me about surprises unless you have it with you to show me immediately." For a mighty conqueror it was so much fun to make him behave like a child. I liked doing this because Alexander had never been allowed much of a childhood. But in our private time I enjoyed being able to give him a fleeting taste of what he should have had. Together with no one around we could act like young carefree boys.

"Perhaps we should wait for me to give it to you. You know, save it for a time when you are less tired and more apt to appreciate it." I continued.

"Hephaestion don't toy with me. You know I love surprises. Well, I love the kind of surprises you give me. Is it another golden medallion with protective Egyptian incantations? Is it a woven leather and linen bridle for Bucephalus?" Alexander quizzed.

"No no nothing like that. This is a totally unique gift unlike any other I have ever given you without really giving it to you." I hinted still giving insufficient information.

"How odd. You say it's a unique gift unlike any other you have ever given me without really giving it to me. I don't know and I'm too tired for mysteries. Nevertheless one more hint." Alexander said encouraging me to continue our childish game.

"It is a part of me but I give it to you so that we might both share what is mine in a way that it will be yours but must always remain mine." I teased him yet further.

"Well that doesn't make any sense. If it is a part of you then it already belongs to me because you are mine." Alexander laughed and clapped his hands. "So your riddle doesn't mean anything."

"Alexander you know that's not fair. You are simplifying it just as you did that Gordian Knot situation." I defended.

"Very well Hephaestion. I have solved it. You have had the Egyptian weavers make a braid from your silky cock hair and it is laced with gold that I might wear it round my neck into battle with me! That my love is my final guess." A smug Alexander smiled at me and made a wide swipe for my ass as we walked from the dining area to our bed chamber.

"Then you give up. Because you are wrong in all that you guess. It is much nicer." I chided him, but I took note of that suggestion and before we left Egypt I had just such a necklace made for him. "There is your gift for tonight dear Alexander." I said pointing toward the door when, as if by command, walked in one of the most beautiful godlike youths that Alexander had ever laid eyes upon. By his color it was obvious he was Greek. Long black curls extended to his shoulders. He was tall for one of his country and his bearing was as regal and aristocratic as any king, except for perhaps Alexander, himself. His eyes, however, were kind and trusting as they surveyed us. His lips were blood red without the benefit of paste and they were full and succulent. His body glistened from the aromatic oil favored by men of those times. His hairless limbs were long and perfectly shaped. This boy/man was completely unclothed. His muscles sleek and well defined from hard work. His cock was long and thick hanging over his ample balls slightly to the left and rooted in a scant nest of ebony black hair. So much of him was a youth and yet there was no mistaking that this was a man. He was perfection.

"Hephaestion, have you drugged me? Is this a vision or have you through the magic of the Egyptian priests made a pact with the gods that one of their own would visit us?" Alexander whispered to me loathe to take his eyes from the object walking toward us.

"Alexander let me present to you Aristenes…my ward." With those words Aristenes bowed and softly said to us. "I am but a servant and yet I stand before my Chiliarch and the god Alexander. What could I ever have done to deserve such honor?"

In the almost two years since I had taken Aristenes as my ward, his development had been remarkable both physically and intellectually. The physical work I had assigned him was variable but apparently very good for him. His muscles were honed so as not to be bulky but were completely evident, especially in the shadowy glow of our torch lit chamber. The dual rows of his washboard abs and chiseled pecs were mouthwatering. His belly button was small and pressed in to almost a vertical slit from the pressure of the tight muscles. The tiny brown nipples belied the sensations they were capable of relaying to his cock and vocal cords by the sweep of a moist tongue and a lightly pressured nibble from my teeth. His body was truly without flaw. I knew this because there was not an inch of his body I had not explored with my eyes, my hands, and my mouth.

While he never complained, I knew that he was not happy that my orders always kept him from the thick of fighting. He yearned to help Alexander, the god-king he had only heard stories about, accomplish his dream of being king of the world. It was my selfishness that prevented him from the battles and possible death. I could not bear the thought of that perfect body being scarred from an enemy's blade or the flesh torn by the cruel penetration of an archer's arrow or his perfectly even teeth being broken in a fight. Each scar that battle had bestowed upon Alexander seemed to add to his beauty and he wore each as a trophy of honor, but I needed something that I could care for and keep beautiful in the bloody violent world I shared with Alexander. Aristenes was my answer. While I did not love him as I loved Alexander, I adored him as a beloved that I must always protect. I had not brought him to Alexander's attention before, because I wanted something that was just mine and that I did not have to share. Certainly, I had mentioned him to Alexander on many occasions and had made him aware that I was going to mentor him. In our time that also meant that I was going to have sex with him. I believe Alexander knew that I wanted to keep him to myself and he never took issue with it. He supported my decision to keep him out of harm's way and never insisted on meeting him. He knew that when I felt the time was right that he would and besides he had way too many things going on to care about what he considered as "my personal project."

I was aware that Aristenes' mind was sharp and thirsting for knowledge. I arranged for him to have the best tutors that were available in our constantly moving entourage. I would have sent him to my own teacher, Aristotle, but that would have meant sending him back to Greece, a thought I could not bear. Already fluent in many of the languages, he was taught how to read and write them as well. Mathematics came easily for him as did all the sciences of the time. Most of his days, while we were in Egypt were spent in its great learning centers, where I was told he devoured everything he could decipher from the ancient hieroglyphics. I also had him schooled in the social graces, thinking that one day I could assign him as one of Alexander's ambassadors, a profession in which I knew he would excel. If Alexander and I had lived longer I have little doubt but that he would have been placed in a position of greatness. Of course, life does not follow the design we lay out for it. Enough digression!

"I have told Alexander about you since before the battle of Tyre. You have learned so much from me and from your teachers. The time is right for you to meet your king that you might also learn from him. I know that he will take to you just as I have. Alexander will no doubt be able to look into your soul and find it as pure and devoted as I have. Alexander! Please pay attention to the introduction!" I chided, noting that Alexander's eyes were locked on my ward's cock.

"What? Yes yes of course no doubt." Alexander stumbled for words as he redirected his attention to Aristenes' face. "The fact is I have heard much about you and value your loyalty. Hephaestion has told me that your knowledge of languages was a great benefit in the assembly of our machines. He also assures me that your value to our empire's future is without estimation. "Alexander was starting to go on and on now that he had regained his royal demeanor.

"Alexander, I have brought you Aristenes as a gift tonight that you might enjoy the pleasure of knowing perfection in its physical form. I must emphasize, however, that I have only done this after speaking to Aristenes and taking into regard his feelings on this matter. While he is our subject and will do as we command, I am the only man he has ever been with in every sense of the word during his lifetime. I asked him if you could be his second." What I was telling Alexander was without precedent. We never asked any man his permission. It was simply assumed that our wish would be obeyed and that anyone would be the better for it.

"And what did your young ward answer to you?" Alexander indulged me.

"Some day in the not too distant future I expect Aristenes to be an important part of our council, so I give him on this night permission to speak freely to us; just as he will have to do when he speaks for us. Tell Alexander your mind Aristenes." I commanded the boy. The three of us were still standing.

"Yes my Chiliarch," responded the young man raising his eyes, which had been looking down in a show of respect, to meet our attentive gaze. "I told the most noble Hephaestion that I would do as he bid. He responded that he wanted me to share openly my feelings about lying with you as I have lain with him. He is all I have ever known and he has taught me all that I know of love with men. I have come to love him with all my heart. I know that my love is not returned in like for he is in love with you and I accept this. I love you as my king and have since I was a boy but I don't love you as I do him, at least not yet. I think I might learn to, because if he loves you so much there must be a reason for it. I know that I feel empty when I lie on my couch and do not have his cock in me. I don't know if I could ever feel that way about you but I can try."

"Well, I don't want to put you out Aristenes." Alexander miffed. I could tell he liked the boy's honesty. In a group situation Alexander would had to display displeasure at this answer, but he honored my request that the boy be candid. He also knew that I would not let this happen if I felt there was any chance of our talk being shared outside our trio.

"Oh Sir, I don't mean to offend!" Aristenes said with the look and uncertainty I noted from our first night together.

"You have not offended boy. I would find it impossible to love anyone as much as him also. But tell me Aristenes would you take my cock and my essence with pleasure? If you will not, I will return Hephaestion's most cherished gift with just the gratitude that it was offered to me at all." Well, I had never heard Alexander talk to anyone like this.

"I will happily spread my cheeks for you my pharaoh. I only have one request if you feel so inclined to hear and possibly grant it." Aristenes stated. Alexander nodded permission to ask. "I will more eagerly receive your cock and swallow your fluid if Hephaestion also be a part of our night."

Alexander looked at me with amusement in his eyes. "You trained him well Hephaestion." I looked at Alexander in denial. "Very well Aristenes. Hephaestion can participate. Come to our bed. I want to see what he has taught you all these months that he has kept you to himself. Remove our robes; my cock has been like a rock since you walked into the room. It would have agreed to your request even if I had not." Aristenes deftly undid the clasp of the robes on both Alexander and me. I watched as they fell to the floor in a fluid motion.

Holding his arms open, Alexander welcomed Aristenes and me into an embrace. First he brought my head over to his and our mouths met before tongue began to duel tongue. My hand bumped into Alexander's as he ran his fingers through the silken curls of the man-boy. Releasing my mouth from his wet probing tongue, Alexander brought Aristenes succulent lips to his own and softly ever so gently introduced the boy to the thrill of being kissed by a king.

I saw that Aristenes' very ample staff had already risen to touch the abdominal skin just below his navel. I had moved in behind him and busied myself with feeling his very hard ass cheeks, every now and then bringing a hand to his front and cupping his large low hanging balls in my palm, all the time nibbling at the nape of his neck. Little gasps came from him and I could feel the prickling of his skin as shivers ran up and down his body from the sensations brought about by the two most powerful men in the world worshiping his body. As Alexander continued to kiss the youth I reached around Aristenes until each of my hands was cupping an ass cheek of the king. Pulling him forward, Alexander's thick cock came into direct contact with Aristenes' powerful manhood and a sigh issued from each of the men.

Knowing what was soon to come and wanting to have Aristenes relaxed, I got down on my knees behind the boy and parted his cheeks. There in front of me was that tight orifice with which I had become so familiar. I brought my face to the crevice of his cheeks and searched out his entrance with my tongue. As always his scent was clean and fresh with only a hint of the usual musty smell of men. I probed the youth as deeply as I could, knowing how much he loved this particular sensation. When he pushed back against my face to get even more of my tongue into him, Alexander noticed the subtle move and released the boy from the kiss and began moving down the smooth chest where he licked and nibbled on the tiny brown nipples until each had grown hard and erect. All the while Aristenes was going from sighs of pleasure to moans of ecstasy. The nipples now almost raw from the assault of the king's teeth now were left abandoned as Alexander licked his way to the tiny slit of a navel. I knew that like I had so many times before, Alexander could feel the boy's silky cock hair tickling his chin as his face pushed the pulsating staff to one side, as he tongued the belly button. I felt Alexander's hands on the back of my head he pulled my face closer in to the boy's ass where my tongue worked furiously to fuck his young tight ass.

Suddenly I heard Aristenes gasp as Alexander, unable to wait any longer, took the young prick into his mouth not stopping until he had reached the thick hairy root.

"My king should you be doing that?" Aristenes choked out, remembering what I had told him regarding the fact that an adult male was expected to never suck a cock. I had told him that a man fucking a youth was fine but that he must never breathe a word that his mentor enjoyed milking his essence from him. I explained to him that it was something that many men did but it was never to be discussed. "It's fine Aristenes. You know the rule." I assured him. With that he relaxed into the back and forth movement of Alexander's continued suction.

While Alexander busied himself with blowing Aristenes, I worked my face between the boy's legs, which I could tell were getting wobbly, and licked his smooth hairless sack. The weight of his large balls on my tongue assured me that he would be able to please the pharaoh.

When I stood up so did Alexander and we both led the young man to our bed. Lying Aristenes into the center of the huge mattress, we each got on one side of him. Alexander was not finished with his magnificent cock and I had yet to kiss him as much as I wanted to. I lay down with my head alongside his and kissed each of his eyes before kissing his lips and taking his lower lip into my mouth and nibbling on it. Alexander's head was at the boy's cock but the agile king had pivoted around so that his cock began demanding to slide between mine and Aristenes' lips. I could feel the semen from Alexander's cock painting our lips as we each began to lick the king's massive pole. We both were now greedily licking and kissing his pulsating cock; our tongues often touching and competing for the gift of his precum. Aristenes was not shy about expressing his pleasure over the king's sucking. While he serviced the boy Alexander was also holding my cock and moving my foreskin over the moist cockhead sending jolts of pleasure throughout my body.

As always it was as if Alexander and I shared thoughts. The king released Aristenes from his oral attentions and crawled over to me. Placing his knees on either side of my chest he offered his cock to my mouth, which I took greedily. Aristenes moved into position and took my own into his mouth. He had become quite the master of the pleasures of fellatio, taking me in his mouth, his lips peeled back my foreskin and in one moist motion he was able to take me down his throat. He was amazing. He provided suction on the downward stroke and yet again on the upward stroke. Sometimes he surprised me by very lightly scraping my shaft with his teeth only to offer a form of apology by swirling his tongue around the underside of the crown, firing every nerve that lay in that delicate area.

"Hephaestion, prepare his ass for me." Alexander whispered. I wasn't surprised by this request. Alexander, knowing my feeling for the boy and how impatient he could be with a first time fuck, was giving me the opportunity to open the tight young Aristenes for his penetration. I was grateful to him for that because the most practiced ass could have trouble accommodating Alexander's girth.

With Aristenes flat on his back, I positioned myself between his legs in a kneeling position. Placing my arms under each of his bent knees, I raised his firm ass up several inches. Alexander had retrieved a bottle of oil and had lathed my dick in it after which he oiled up his thick thumb and pushed it into Aristenes' young hole. I heard him gasp at the intrusion but he soon relaxed. His eyes were like depthless black pools as they locked on my own eyes and I felt Alexander guide my cock to his waiting canal. I remember the chiseled jaws on his face tense when he felt the bluntness of my head forcing its way into him. I pushed quickly to shorten the always present pain of my entry. Once the head of my cock was past his muscle ring, his face visibly relaxed, and after just a few seconds I pushed in steadily until I felt my balls resting against him. I began my thrusts slowly then quickened my pace and then slow again, thrilling at the moist tightness. Alexander was now standing with his legs wide apart and had put his cock back in my mouth for me to nurse while I fucked Aristenes. The slap of my now sweaty balls against his ass could be heard throughout the room as could the moans of the deep voiced young man. No longer able to see his eyes, because Alexander's pubic nest blocked my view, I could feel his hands on each of my thighs rubbing against my leg hair. I felt my balls contract into my body. It was now out of my control as my seed almost painfully made its way up my shaft and shot load after load into that ever so tight hole. Even after coming I continued to pump and I could feel my sperm leaking out of his ass and onto my ball sac. Not wanting to force all of my seed from his ass I pulled out with a wet sucking plop and with my fist I squeezed the last few drops from my staff and used my sensitive cockhead to rub the glistening white milk drops on Aristenes smooth balls.

Alexander had felt his own balls ascending and had pulled from my mouth and just watched the two of us finish our fuck. "Hephaestion do you think he is ready for me?"

"As ready as he will ever be Alexander." I told him and gave an encouraging smile to Aristenes, who was staring at Alexander's cock which now looked bigger than ever. The head was almost purple and the shaft was enormous with large veins throughout. I had moved aside after lowering Aristenes legs and was quickly replaced by Alexander, who quickly hoisted the boy's ass up onto his golden fleeced thighs. Just as Alexander had done for me, I oiled his cock generously. I did not however put oil into the boy's ass, knowing that my seed was still lining him in copious amounts and should provide him with more than enough lubrication.

Typical Alexander, for no more had I placed the tip of his cock against the boy-man's arse than the king pushed forward. The boy had once again locked his eyes on mine and I saw the wince of pain at the same time I saw the head of Alexander's cock disappear followed rapidly by his entire shaft. Fortunately, my own not too shabby girth and my seed had prepared him for an Alexander the Great fuck. The moans began immediately being issued from the youth as his penetrator pummeled that tight ass hitting his prostate with every thrust. Alexander was completely oblivious to everything but the tightness around his cock. Aristenes was writhing and the sounds of pleasure were getting louder. This went on for probably twenty minutes before a sweating and out of breath king shot his royal load to mix with mine in what had to be the most beautiful ass in the entire world.

Just as I had done the first time, Alexander sat there for a time with his cock encased in the young Greek. Alexander pulled out of him with his prick glistening from the combination of our two ejaculations. Aristenes had never taken his eyes from me but lay there with a satisfied look on his face. But the boy's cock was still unspent and twitching with a need for release. Alexander and I both looked at each other and smiled. The king was the first to go down on Aristenes swallowing the youth's manhood to the root and twirling his tongue around the shaft each time he pulled up to the sensitive head and probed the opening. While Alexander, whom I admit was quite the expert, gave head I lay between the young man's spread legs and licked that velvet smooth sac luxuriating in its taste and texture. This boy was ready to explode, he was wiggling beneath us crying, smiling, and laughing all at the same time as we administered this exquisite pleasure pain to him. When I felt his loaded testicles retract I lifted my lips from his now tight wrinkled scrotum. The king had his hand around Aristenes' cock, holding it at a ninety degree angle from the boy's bush, and with his mouth slightly open and still flicking his tongue against the now excruciatingly sensitive head with my lips opposite Alexander's we waited with eager anticipation for what we knew was coming. A loud deep guttural sound came from Aristenes as every muscle in that beautiful body went rigid and spurt after spurt of thick white seed shot from the boy. Alexander and I both were doing our best to use our tongues and lips to drink the man's essence. We were both getting our fill but still what we missed was getting in our hair and even our eyes.

Satiated we collapsed, one of us on each side of this delectable young man.

I don't know how long we slept, but at some point I was awakened by a rhythmic movement. Alexander had turned Aristenes on to his side and fed his cock once more the boy's well used whole. The motion that had awakened me was the slow thrusting of the king into that tight ass. The boy was watching me and smiling as his king used his body to pleasure himself. I moved my head toward him and we kissed until Alexander had reached his climax and withdrew. Aristenes, having felt my manhood once more aroused, turned to his other side, reached back and gently guided me into him. Alexander gently kissed him, while I placed my hand on the young warrior's staff and pulled him closer to my thrusting. I don't remember pulling out of him. We slept soundly until morning when Alexander summoned slaves to our room to wash the three of us. I wondered if the slave washing Alexander's face noticed the dried cum streak down his cheek? If he did, he was smart enough not to give any indication.

Chapter Seven
Persian Campaign Continue

Having stayed in Egypt for only a little over a year enjoying the wealth and beauty of this ancient kingdom, we marched eastward in the spring of 331 BC into Mesopotamia and defeated Darius once more at the Battle of Gaugamela. We chased Darius as far as Arbela where the ruined king managed to flee over the mountains to Ecbatana.

It is worthy of mention here, when Darius fled from battle a couple of years earlier, that he left his mother, wife, and daughters behind. Not to mention a vast treasury. It seems that so sure of victory was Darius, that he had brought along fifteen great wagons of treasure including family and friends. Upon his fleeing and the subsequent capture of both his treasury and family word got to Alexander and me that the wife and daughters of Darius were wailing uncontrollably at the supposed death of Darius as well as fear for their own lives. We knew that as women they presented little threat to us but that as members of long lineage of royals they did have clout with the Persian people and therefore presented us with opportunity. We set up a meeting with the women scheduled for later that day.

I was the first to arrive in the tent, where the women still cowered weeping, with Alexander about ten seconds behind me. The queen groveled before me and began begging for the lives of her and her daughters and raving on and on about how magnificent I looked. Of course she was only confirming what I already knew. Well, all worshiping has to end eventually as did this when one of the guards advised the queen that I was not Alexander. Mortified at her mistake the queen immediately switched her attention to Alexander crying and begging forgiveness because of her stupidity. Alexander's response to her was been retold thousands of times over the years. "Do not lament. You were not mistaken for he also is Alexander." I don't think I ever loved him quite as much as I did in that instant when he declared publicly that he and I were as one. We assured the women that not only would their lives be spared but that their lifestyles would not change and they would be accorded all the respect due their royal station. They were all to be housed in their former palace.

As I said that had been two years earlier even before Tyre was taken, Alexander had received a letter from Darius. The Persian king proposed ten thousand talents ransom for the captured ladies of his family and offered Alexander all Persian territory west of the Euphrates, together with the hand of his daughter in marriage. To which Alexander replied that he already possessed and controlled the territory in question and that he was free to marry Darius's daughter with or without her father's consent.

This was Alexander's opportunity to march forward and capture the fabled city of Babylon. This we did with little resistance. This was a city of magnificence. Full of architectural wonders that are spoken of yet today, we fell in love with everything about it. Unfortunately our time here was much too short. Perhaps I will elaborate on Babylon later.

From Babylon, Alexander went to Susa, one of the Achaemenid capitals, to capture its legendary treasury. This was done with relative ease. Then, sending most of his army to the Persian ceremonial capital of Persepolis via the Royal Road, Alexander and I took our own select troops on the direct route to the city. We had to storm the pass of the forbidding Persian Gates, which was blocked by a Persian army under Ariobarzanes and then make a dash for

Persepolis before its guards could loot the treasury for themselves.

Such wealth we could not even fathom. Chamber upon chamber of gold molded not only into Persian coins but also into the likeness of gods and animals. Some of the latter weighed so much that it took many men to move them. In other rooms, casket upon casket of precious gems that had been polished to such a gleam that the light from only one torch was reflected in a kaleidoscope of color about the chamber. As rich as the coffers of Egypt had been, it was but a poor neighbor to this very advanced empire.

We stayed for a while in Persepolis. Not only to rest, but to watch over the score of treasury accountants given the task of cataloguing the wealth and oversee the journey of much of it back to our home country of Macedon. We also needed some time to gather our generals and discuss future plans. There was after all still more of the empire to absorb and we could not forget that Darius was still very much alive. Also, Alexander was in the mood for a party such as only he could host.

We treated Susa and Persepolis differently than we had many other conquests. In general, Alexander and I decided to try a somewhat novel idea and be beneficent with the Persians as a whole. I had little trouble in persuading Alexander into doing this. For one thing as much as he enjoyed destruction he also enjoyed beauty and creation. Persia offered beauty in its cities, its dress, its customs, and its men. I can still remember how upset Alexander became when fire broke out in the eastern palace of Xerxes and spread to the rest of the city.

What we did differently with the Persians was to not only let them keep their customs but we also adopted some of theirs, to the chagrin of many of our own men. We encouraged our soldiers to take Persian wives. We let the religious practices continue and both Alexander and I would garb in Persian vestments at ceremonial occasions. We did not put all the men to death, with the exception of high ranking army officers. Nor did we torture, again with the exception of those who we considered a threat.

The leaders of this city who decided to recognize Alexander as their king remained in their political positions. The only difference was that now they paid their allegiance to Alexander. It was with this understanding and the fact that the community leaders were not put to death that they decided to throw a great celebration for Alexander. While somewhere in the mountainous wilderness of Persia, King Darius was fleeing for his life, the people of Persepolis were preparing a great feast in the grand hall of Darius's former palace. Life is full of irony!

Exotic fruits were laid out as were breads of unusual grains. Enormous vessels of rare wine lined the wall with scores of servants with the understanding that there would be dire consequences if Alexander or any of his company would find themselves with empty goblet. Pigs, cattle, lambs, and all sorts of fowl were roasted and made succulent with unknown aromatic spices and laid upon the ornate tables before the king and his men. Dancers whose numbers were made up of beautiful women and young men who were even more physically beautiful than their female counterparts, performed choreography from Persian folk dance to graphic sexual acts set to the beat of drums.

It is here that I must confide to you the fact that the great

Alexander was well on his way to becoming a sot. He had always enjoyed drinking alcohol. While I enjoyed wine and looked for bouquet, Alexander enjoyed anything that made him drunk. The stress of world conquest, betrayal, death and the search for pleasure all combined with unbridled power took its toll on my love. Lines that should not have been visible at his early age were becoming evident on his beautiful visage. Had he lived but a full decade longer his beauty would have turned wrinkled and bloated and his great mind would have become befuddled. I had saved him from no few misjudgments. Some days were spent entirely on recovering from the previous night. As in all things related to the life of Alexander, moderation was neither sought nor tolerated.

So it was with the mixture of endless wine, erotic dances, the beating of drums, and the hypnotic movement of torch flames casting layers of shadows about the hall that I noticed Alexander rubbing his crotch through the heavily brocaded Persian robe he had worn to the event. Alexander had caught my look and was smiling at me. I returned his look and with a negative shake of my head found myself smiling back. Well, it had been a long and stressful journey and the thought of recreational sex was very appealing. Besides, I was feeling my wine and would have not been able to stop the events of the evening if I had been so inclined.

The orgy spread like a plain's grass fire, once it got started. You must remember the banquet hall was filled with two primary groups. Although mixed together there was the conquered and the conqueror. Of course I do not count the slaves, who were brought into the mix simply because they were slaves. Alexander's first move was to reach over and draw my face to his for a kiss. He must not have been as drunk as I thought since this was a wise act on his part. We were all sitting on plush floor cushions with our legs crossed before the banquet tables. Next he lifted his robe to waist level and not wearing anything else his huge cock was quite visible resting over his smooth silken ball bag. The eyes of everyone near enough trained in on that magnificent piece of manhood, with its bush of golden curlies glinting in the torch light. The men of our army having seen their king in his glory before smiled appreciatively while the Persian men and their women, who had rarely if ever seen such light hair, simply stared, not knowing exactly how they should act.

Let me interject here that while Alexander's sexual preferences were well known, many of the Persian men with us this evening were not as comfortable displaying themselves for public view. These men, however, had welcomed leadership change from the regimented former king's style to that of a young visionary. It was that mindset that had spared their lives and placed them in the army of Macedon with their ranks intact. Besides, what better way to introduce them to the Alexander way of doing things? You might want to look at it as a form of your modern day fraternal haze system. Let us get back to retelling our party story.

Alexander had focused his attentions on a young and beautiful Persian captain by the name of Artachshatra, whose name meant great warrior in Old Persian. Artachshatra had attended the gathering with his wife of only two months. A beautiful young woman of perhaps nineteen years to her husband's twenty years, she was seated at a lower elevation than the men, as were all the women. While it was known that women would really not have anything significant to contribute to the conversation of a group of men, it was out of respect that she and other wives were seated close enough as to be privy to what was taking place. Artachshatra was at a complete loss as to why Alexander had exposed his genitals and was looking at him. Alexander gently took the young captain's hand and brought it over to his semi flaccid penis. I saw the cock twitch at the touch of the captain.

The room had become suddenly quiet and Artachshatra was the focus of every Persian and Greek in the hall. The Persians were watching for the reaction of the young hero who had proven himself time and again on the battlefield and one who had conducted his life in a conservative heterosexual lifestyle. The Greek soldiers, who mostly preferred women but certainly were not opposed to same sex satiation, were watching Artachshatra to see just how loyal he really was to their beloved Alexander. To say you could hear a pin drop in the chamber might be an exaggeration but the room was heavy with anticipation. This situation could go in one of two directions and there was no way of knowing which way it would go.

Artachshatra did not pull his hand back from the king's growing cock but did continue to look at Alexander eye to eye and he was not returning the king's sparkling smile. Alexander gave a slight nod of his head to the captain and waited. Hell we were all waiting. I really didn't want to see the soldier end up dead. He was truly beautiful. A head full of thick black hair, eyes of deep ebony, eyebrows that arched in a masculine way as if he was truly interested in what you said to him, had not grown a beard yet over a fabulous chiseled jaw, and his nose while not his most prominent feature had a slight curve to it in the Persian manner. His body was olive in tone and muscular but not muscle bound. In other words this guy would make almost anyone's mouth water.

The impasse came to an end when Artachshatra wrapped his fingers partially around Alexander's now hard dick, held it up and with the index finger of his left hand swept it over the tip of the king's leaking cock and bringing it to his lips suckled on it and smiled. There is little wonder that this man had made the rank of captain at such an early age. Alexander laughed uproariously. I began to clap and soon everyone was applauding in approval. Except for perhaps the captain's wife, who along with the other women were escorted from the hall, but not before an over the shoulder glance at her new husband discovered him removing his robe. The servant girls and the dancers were the only women left in the hall and they were there for the pleasure of the men who found such activity pleasurable.

With Alexander and Captain Artachshatra having led the way men everywhere were disrobing and grabbing whatever man they chose. Some men had paired up and were fucking the servant girls. One muscular hairy soldier had lain on his side and had buried his cock into the tight pussy a young slave girl of perhaps eight-teen and a smooth bronzed Persian had lain behind her and slid his long narrow staff in alongside the Greek officer. As they fucked her, their cocks rubbed against each other in such pleasure that both were moaning and each had the others ass cupped in their hand.

Meanwhile, I chose to watch. I love watching former enemies come to terms. So I decided to just sit for a while, eat melon, and drink wine. Alexander had pulled the captain from his now very rigid cock and was kissing him full in the mouth. This was not something that Macedonians supported but this was Alexander who had not only given them victory but also wealth, so some of his activities were simply dismissed. The Persian officer now with no clothing on at all except for a wide gold bracelet was truly a sight to behold. His thighs were roped with muscle and he had beautifully shaped calves. His torso, as were his legs, was dusted in fine short black hair. He had a distinct trail of silken hair running from below his well-chiseled pectorals to a thick black bush of pubic hair. Here the hair was long, glistening with his natural oils, and curly. In fact there was so much hair that it grew a ways up the base of his thick long penis. His ball sac was devoid of hair and looked like a great silken bag. He was not as big as Alexander or me, for that matter, at probably seven inches it had a perfect curve with a head that was ridged just right for a variety of uses.

Alexander was luxuriating now with his back against a pillow in a semi sitting position; his legs slightly spread apart and sipping wine while he enjoyed Artachshatra sucking him. Every now and then the young soldier would falter because of his inexperienced gag reflex, but he was quickly learning the art of fellatio. Alexander scooted himself up to where his back was almost upright and pulling the captain's head off his turgid cock he once more kissed his lips and this time being the alpha type fighter he was I noticed that it was his tongue probing Alexander's mouth.

I felt the captain's kiss lasted a little longer than necessary for someone who just thirty minutes earlier professed to only like sex with women. But an experience like he was having with Alexander made it quite understandable. Alexander pulled back from the kiss. Both of their lips were glossy from the shared spittle of that deep kiss. Artachshatra somewhat out of breath looked questionably at Alexander. "Why had the king stopped," him he was thinking? What I saw from my vantage point sitting next to Alexander was the sovereign's massive cock still wet from being sucked by the novice and jerking impatiently against his belly. Artachshatra, upright on his knees to the left of Alexander with his long slender cock pointing slightly to the left of his navel, was soon to find out why the kiss had been interrupted. Alexander grabbing his own dick but only able to get his hand a little over half way around its base nodded his head to the handsome captain. Again that perplexed look from Artachshatra. Then suddenly his eyes lit with fear. Alexander was ordering him to sheath his cock in his virgin ass!

Knowing better than to disobey even a nonverbal order from the king the handsome young officer stood and placing his feet to either side of Alexander began to squat down with his back to the king. "No Artachshatra I want you facing me while I fuck you." Alexander told him while all the time smiling at him.

"Yes my king," Artachshatra immediately responded and shifted position. "But sir I must beg your mercy and consideration in realizing that I find myself in unfamiliar territory. Please extend to me help and your divine patience." The young man pleaded respectfully. Without answering, Alexander ordered a slave to lathe his prick with oil from the table and placing his hands on each of the beautiful warrior's lightly haired golden toned thighs, assisted him as he lowered himself down lower and lower to imminent pain.

The soldier placed his hands on each of Alexander's shoulders for additional balance as he squatted down over the royal fuck pole. I remained watching impassively as the hitherto untouched rosebud came in contact with the head of Alexander's cock. Artachshatra sucked in a quick breath as Alexander moved his hands from the ropy muscles of his thighs and placed them on his waist. I don't know if it was out of drunkenness or just cruelty on Alexander's part, but in one sudden thrust the king's cock breached the virgin hole and entered completely. The young commander screamed in absolute agony. Too much the soldier to sob, tears were never the less streaming from his eyes and cascading down his perfect face.

The room had become quiet at the sound of what was obviously a cry of torture. Alexander remained very still but continued smiling at the captain. As for the officer he remained in too much pain to move and so just sat on his knees with his hairy calves resting against either side of Alexander's furry thighs.

"Party people! He is fine," reassured Alexander. As if on cue everybody went back to fucking, sucking, kissing, and drinking. The young captain's plight was all but forgotten by his lust-crazed comrades.

For no less than five minutes Alexander stroked the man-boy's chest and face. Assuring him that the sudden thrust and the pain was much less searing then a slow penetration would have been. Artachshatra's facial expression did not look convinced but he nodded his head in agreement anyway. Smart soldier. One never wanted to outright disagree with Alexander when he was in the drink. Soon Alexander was giving little thrusts in the man's hole and pressing at an angle he knew would be hitting that sweet button. Soon enough Artachshatra was pushing himself up and down. The pleasure was beginning to override the pain of his torn asshole.

"Hephaestion help me make amends for my rude breach of our young Persian's love canal." Alexander demanded of me with a smile.

"Of course sire. What would you suggest to remedy this unfortunate situation?" I asked.

"Why suck his cock! Yes suck his cock while I fuck him." Alexander laughed.

I shot a look of complete surprise and tried to feign discomfort toward Alexander. But I was actually thinking to myself that it had taken him way too long to ask me to do my part in this little planned scenario. Alexander and I had both discussed the potential of this new rising star in our army. I slowly got up on my knees and looked Artachshatra directly in his ebony eyes. As I moved into position I remember feeling the moistness in my own hole from the several squirts of sperm placed there earlier by Alexander. I smiled reassuringly at him and stroked his shoulder. Leaning down toward his long penis I quickly glanced at Alexander just long enough to wink at him and then I had the captain's silk smooth penis in my mouth. While I generally would not suck dick in a public forum I knew that having been ordered to do so by the King of Kings would not reflect negatively on me, but would rather appear that I was a Greek Chiliarch forcing a sexual perversion on a former enemy. As a result of the pain he had so recently experienced his penis was now only semi flaccid and I was able to take the whole of the spongy appendage into my mouth and swirl my tongue around it quickly bringing it back to rigidity. Soon I had an up and down rhythm going so that when I went all the way down on the Persian's leaking cock my chin was hitting Alexander's abdomen as he thrust up repeatedly plunging his cock into the man's ass. This went on for probably ten minutes. I know my jowls had begun to burn from the constant sucking when Captain Artachshatra suddenly went tense and blew a wad that filled my mouth. It was a savory and rich cream that reminded me a great deal of the Persian diet. I lost very little of his ejaculate and rising up I crushed my lips to his and forced him to taste for the first time his own spunk mixed with my spit. I then moved to Alexander and kissing my king deeply, shared the young man's cum which was now mixed with not only his saliva but also mine. Alexander sucked my tongue greedily. A few more thrusts and the king forced the soldier off his cock with a loud wet plop and told him to start sucking that monolith that had just been pumping his ass. Artachshatra obliged and Alexander came in great torrents down his throat. I might note here that Artachshatra not only did not lose a drop of the royal essence but also had to be asked to quit sucking. The Persian captain would certainly have a sore ass for the next few days and probably even be spotting blood for several hours but he was now a convert. From that night on I am sure that his times in battle encampments were much less lonely. In fact, I remember mentioning to Alexander during our Indian campaign that I had noticed a youthful slave enter the officer's tent each night. Change is often a good thing.

You might wonder what I thought about my man having sex with different partners. The answer is simple but also complicated. I didn't like it at all. In fact I was terribly jealous. I honestly think I could have been monogamous with him. But at the same time I knew how Alexander's mind worked. If I had been that demanding for his complete affections I would never have had a life with him at all. He was very much a man with sexual needs and desires as in truth was I. It would be an outright lie for me to deny enjoying some of the sexual benefits I enjoyed due to Alexander. We were often parted for extended periods of time. Who would choose to pleasure himself all the time when surrounded with literally thousands of willing (or sometimes unwilling) partners at his command? Besides by my participating in activities like this or with just a third person I was able to watch Alexander and I could tell if the sex was recreational or sincere. Just as my sex with Aristenes was a need to fill loneliness so for the most part was Alexander's lust. Not to say that I didn't carry on about it from time to time, but I knew he needed the taste of another man's cock or the feel of another ass to fuck. Now, two thousand three hundred years later, I can publicly admit that when I found out Alexander was repeatedly having sex with the same person I was not above having him transferred to another part of the empire or promoting him to the front lines where almost certain death or disfigurement was his fate. Not that I am a petty sort. I like to think I was protective of my interests. In the end it was always me he came back to and that dear reader was what made all the difference.

Chapter Eight
Rid of Darius at Last

After a brief respite in Persepolis, Alexander and I decided it was time to set off in pursuit of Darius again, first into Media, and then Parthia. By this time the invincible army of Darius was fractured beyond reparation. The Persian monarch's troops, both humiliated and defeated, were loath to remain united under their king. Darius was taken prisoner by Bessus, his Bactrian satrap as well as being a relative of the king. Upon our army's approach, Bessus had his men fatally stab the king and proceeded to declare himself Darius' successor as Artaxwerxes V, before retreating into Central Asia to launch a guerrilla campaign against us. Alexander reacted to the murder of Darius much differently than people expected by having the remains of the Persian king buried next to his Achaemenid processors in a full regal funeral befitting a deceased monarch. Alexander also claimed that, while dying, Darius had named him as his successor to the Achaemenid throne. Was this last a true claim? Well let me say that it was a good PR move and certainly fodder for the masses.

With Alexander now convinced that he was the legitimate successor to Darius, we now viewed Bessus as a usurper to the Achaemenid throne, and so with little ado we set out to put an end to him. As with everything concerning my beloved, this campaign, originally planned as a short chase and capture of Bessus, evolved into a grand tour of central Asia, with Alexander founding several new cities. And surprise! All of these new cities were called Alexandria, including but not limited to modern Kandahar in Afghanistan, and Alexandria Eschate in the modern area of Tajikistan. The campaign took us through Media, Parthia, Aria, and Scythia.

In around 329 BC karma caught up with Bessus, who was betrayed by Spitamenes, a person little is known about except that he was part of the satrapy of Sogdiana. In what, I am sure was planned as a smart move, Spitamenes handed over Bessus to Ptolemy, one of Alexander's trusted generals, and Bessus was summarily executed without much ado. Unfortunately, Spitamenes, not being able to leave well enough alone raised Sogdiana in revolt. Alexander was livid and immediately launched a campaign against Spitamenes and defeated him in the Battle of Gabai. Following the trend of the time, Spitamenes was killed by his own men, who then, wisely sued for peace.

It was around this time that a couple of glitches came about. One was the clash of cultures between what was considered etiquette by the Persians and what was considered ridiculous by our Macedonians. Alexander had decided to take the Persian title Shahanshah ("King of Kings") as well as adopting other elements of Persian dress and customs at his court. The most objectionable to the Macedonians was the custom of proskynesis, which could be either a symbolic kissing of the hand or prostration on the ground. Proskynesis was a gesture of respect to one's social superiors. Naturally, Alexander preferred the throwing of one's self on the ground to kissing his ring. The Greeks regarded this act as something only performed for deities and some believed that Alexander meant to formally deify himself by requiring it. This cost him the respect of many of his countrymen. In fact so much unhappiness resulted that a plot on his life was revealed. As a result one of his officers, Philotas, was executed for failing to bring the plot to his attention. This then necessitated the execution of the officer's father, Parmenion who had been left in charge of guarding the treasury at Ecbatana, so that he might not seek vengeance for the death of his son. Later a second plot on his life was revealed and found to have been instigated by his own royal pages. Also implicated in this second plot was our personal historian, Callisthenes of Olynthus, who had vehemently opposed proskynesis. To top all of this, the constant accumulation of power and unimaginable wealth had significantly contributed to Alexander drinking himself into disturbing periods of drunkenness on an almost daily basis. These disastrous public displays would often manifest themselves in fits of rage. Where at one time Alexander would not only tolerate but encourage his officers and friends to argue and disagree with him over various decisions, he now considered himself to be above reproach. In one of his most infamous recorded acts, Alexander personally slew the man who had saved his life at Granicus, Cleitus the Black, during a drunken argument at Maracanda.

But ultimately it was I who suffered the most from his constant reveries. More and more frequently Alexander would lay almost comatose while I tried to rouse him with my mouth to no avail. Sometimes out of frustration I would roll him onto his stomach and fuck him a few times a night and in return only get a few grunts out of him. But I still loved him and wanted to help him. On a regular basis I also thanked the gods for Aristenes!

The second glitch in this time period was that when the final Persian surrender came about, the defeated army showered the former treasures of Darius upon Alexander (that is what treasure we had not already taken). Included in this effort for leniency was a eunuch named Bagoas. He had been the property of Darius and was of truly exceptional beauty. It was said that Darius fucked Bagoas as often as his wife or any of his concubines. He had been recognized at a very young age for his magnificent looks and trained since almost an infant in the harem of the Persian king. Supposedly his talent for pleasing men was without male or female peer. This made me none too happy since I knew what a sucker (no pun intended) Alexander was for anything that made him feel good.

Bagoas apparently had good management, who knew how to promote him. There was one festive night when a huge victory party was thrown in, of course, Alexander's honor. There was music and dancing. Among the dancers was Bagoas who performed a very erotic number that captured every man's attention. Naturally Bagoas won the competition and was invited to sit beside Alexander. The Macedonian soldiers were so beside themselves with the eunuch's performance that they kept applauding and yelling for Alexander to kiss him. (I was not pleased.) At long last (maybe four seconds) Alexander capitulated and drew Bagoas in for a long and tender kiss. This thrilled the Greeks no end, especially since it was a direct affront to me. Without elaboration, let me just say, that when Alexander was not too much into his cup, he fucked the asshole of his balless eunuch from that night forward. The eunuch as well as Roxanna, Alexander's wife taken not long after, became part of our caravan and a big part of my resentment. Both were trouble-makers.

Roxanna was the daughter of a Sogdian nobleman who had valiantly defended his mountain fortress against us. Upon his defeating the Sogdians, Alexander knew the importance of banning the chieftain groups into a cohesive unit under his authority and so it was decided that he would marry Roxanna, daughter of the chieftain. Some historians note that next to the widow of Darius III, she was the most beautiful woman in the empire. In my opinion, while not ugly, she bordered on having a peasant's figure and a face too broad for most men's appeal. Had she lived long enough I am sure that my theories about her looks would have become fact.

The wedding was a necessity and I did my part as Alexander's best friend. It went off without a hitch as you people say. I knew her purpose and I knew that it was me Alexander loved. So it was what it was. Roxanna was the first wife. Alexander would eventually marry the daughter of Darius in his effort to found a strong dynasty. That marriage I was not happy with either. In fact I was never happy with his getting married. In front of the troops I was a total macho man, but behind closed doors (or tent flaps) I could be a complete drama queen.

Needless to say, Roxanna and I were oil and water. We hated each other intensely. Probably the only thing we shared was a common hatred of Bagoas. Outside of wishing them well on the night of their wedding, I can't recall having ever said anything to her. It was with satisfaction that more times than not I would send her husband to her empty of seed while I felt full of his essence. I smile even now at the memory. How many times, I wonder, did Roxanna try without success to rouse the cock of her husband who was already spent and usually inebriated? I am sure she noticed that the cap of his huge shaft still dribbled semen as she stroked it and certainly she couldn't miss my ejaculate that had dried trapped in his treasure trail. How she must have hated me! Unfortunately, I was not always in town. Somehow, the persistent Roxanna caught my man at the right time and she eventually gave birth to Alexander's son.

The memory of that first wedding still pisses me off. So I will finish that narrative. Alexander had put on a great wedding feast in his and Roxanna's honor. It was an event in which I was expected to participate. I laughed, I smiled, I did everything the best friend is supposed to do. I stood in my place of honor behind the bride and groom where I was forced to endure a panoramic view of the bride's fat ass for over an hour. I managed to excuse myself from the reception after offering the perfunctory toast to the couple's future happiness.

About an hour later, alone, angry, and hurt in my rooms, I was surprised to see Alexander coming none too happily in my bedchamber. Actually, I wasn't too surprised. As his most trusted friend I had been expected to stay near his side throughout the fete.

"What the fuck are you doing sequestered in your rooms when your duty is to be with me?" The blushing groom demanded of me.

"My apologies," I said to him. "I have an excruciating headache and wanted to rest momentarily." I know! I know! It wasn't very original twenty-three centuries ago either.

"A headache my fucking ass!" he said in a louder than necessary voice. Putting his arm around my shoulder and pulling me close to him he advised, "I need you Hephaestion. I need your support in front of my army. I need you to bless this union and be happy for me." He actually stated this last with a serious face.

As unhappy as I was that my friend and lover had married, I knew that I owed him my support. At the same time I dreaded standing in that great palace hall and giving blessing after blessing to his marriage. There were a few reasons for this. One, I did not enjoy the thought of sharing him officially with anyone and second I knew there were Macedonean soldiers that viewed my position with disfavor and now felt that this marriage to a woman would erode my influence with Alexander. Certainly, there was also a twinge of jealousy on my part. I felt that I should have been the one exchanging vows of allegiance with Alexander. That, however, was not a possibility then and twenty-three centuries later is still not truly accepted. There are some enlightened countries and some liberal states in America that have made it legal but it's fragile and a change in government whim or a resurgence of the disease of religion and it will be taken away once again.

"Very well Alexander. If I must then I will do it. I will go down there with you and smile and look happy for you. I will toast to you and your bride's future and plead to the gods on your behalf that you have a houseful of heirs. I will not reveal that all the while I feel like I am toasting away my future happiness. This is, after all, your day." I said in my best "no matter how much you hurt me I am always here for you" voice.

"Hephaestion must we go through this again today of all days? Your future is in no way affected. You are truly my consort, not her. We make love to each other as equals, we go into battle side by side, maybe to die together, and you are the only man in my empire who can speak for me. What more can I do? Would you like to share my wife with me? I don't care if our child is mine or yours. You can share our bed this very night. I will tell her this...."

"No!No! That won't be necessary." I quickly informed him. My stomach almost turning over at the mere thought of sticking my cock into the mushy belly of his wife.

"Then by the gods what do you want me to do?" An exasperated Alexander asked.

"Let me fuck you. I want to fuck you right now with you in your marriage robe. I want you to do exactly as I ask with no questions."

"Very well. I am at your service if that will get you back to the hall to perform your duties. We must hurry however. I don't want her getting an attitude as well."

In all my years with Alexander I had never played this role. I figured I had about fifteen minutes to fulfill my fantasy, so there was no time to waste.

"Get on your knees in front of me!" Alexander gave me a surprised look but did as I bid. It was a strange sight. Never in our many years had Alexander been the first one to get on his knees in front of me to do what was obviously next to be done. I had been in this position hundreds of times and loved every minute of it. I lifted the plush brocaded red and gold robe up to just under my shoulders and brought my rigid manhood out from the confines of my thong. Ordering Alexander to open his mouth, I peeled back my foreskin and thrust my cock deep into his beautiful face. Immediately, his tongue went to work. His licking around my corona tickled and the tip of his tongue felt as if he was trying to gain entry into my piss slit, then down into his throat my cock went. I was leaking semen like crazy and the sound of him lapping at it was quite audible. After a while I pulled out of his mouth and ordered him to lick my balls. He was so incredibly good at that.

"Good little boy." I told him and patted his head. I didn't know how he was going to take that but he lifted his gaze up to me as if to say what next. He actually had a sweet little smile.

"Go to my desk and lean over it." I commanded. Alexander did as he was told. I walked up behind him pulled his robe up to just over his lower back and in the flick of my wrist his thong fell below his knees. His beautiful ass with its golden fleece filled crack lay before me. I spit in my hand slicked up my cock and drove it all the way in with one thrust. Alexander started to cry out in pain but then caught himself. I let my shaft lay in his depths luxuriating in the magnificent warmth and tightness. I widened my stance and got a good grip on his sides for better balance and started pummeling his ass harder then I had ever done. I did it because at that moment I hated him as much as I loved him. With every inward thrust he grunted but I could feel him pushing back to get even more of my cock into him. For ten minutes I fucked out my frustration for having to share him with that woman. The fucking was becoming more audible and was slurppy moist. I could feel the rub of his prostate against me and he was wiggling his ass side to side in an attempt to gain even more sensation from my invading rod. His stomach, down against my desk, was becoming slick with sweat. Suddenly my Shahanshah gasped for air, groaned, grabbed the edge of the desk and tensed as he shot strand after strand of his heir makers onto the floor. He had come without so much as touching his beautiful mouthwatering cock. My own orgasm was close at hand after all of that. One more solid thrust in that gripping hot tunnel smashed my cock hair against the royal ass and I impaled my king as deeply as I could. I began firing my seed into that tight warm canal. When my spasms had almost ended I pulled out quickly and finished shooting two thick wads into the palm of my hand. I leaned over my lover's back and placing the palm of my hand at his mouth told him to lick the pearlescent pool from me. I then drew him back toward me, turned him around, and we kissed deeply. My tongue sharing the taste of my seed with him made all the hate and jealousy vanish. Secure in the knowledge that he would be fucking his bride with my sperm gushing around in his guts and its flavor on the back of his tongue I smiled at him.

"That was nice. I'm now ready to go back with you." I told him. He just stood there staring at me as I helped straighten his robe. In helping him to do this I confess I did squeeze his cock and managed to secure a few drops of fluid which I licked with relish from my fingers. I offered him my arm and we walked back toward the banquet hall leaving his thong lying on the floor by the desk. But I knew he would make me pay later for my demands. I could hardly wait.

Chapter Nine
To India

Proceeding with our boyhood plans, Alexander and I decided to head on to the mysterious land of India. I just didn't feel as confident about this campaign as I had the others. As a result I had Aristenes placed in charge of our palace with orders that he was to continue his studies under the battery of instructors I had brought from Egypt as well as those commissioned from Greece and Persia. I could not bear the thought of our ambitions bringing harm to this loyal young man. I made up my mind that, should I live, I would secure a title for him, house him in his own grand villa, and bestow enough wealth that he would never have want.

So in the spring of 327 BC, we took our army into India, and Alexander divided his forces. He led his section north into the Swat Valley, while I took a large contingent through the Khyber Pass. My mission was to take over either by force or agreement all places through which my march took me, and on reaching the Indus I was to make suitable preparations for crossing. I was certainly in unfamiliar territory, with no knowledge what so ever of the political and geographical landscapes. I had to make decisions on the spot. I reached the Indus with the land behind me conquered, including the successful siege of Peuceolatis, which took us a full thirty days. I immediately began to organize the construction of boats for crossing this great river.

Overall, India was quite grueling. I had men dying from strange fevers. There were insects that bit us and sucked our blood. Snakes of mythological proportions and some that while not so big their bite would kill a warrior in minutes. We conquered every kingdom we encountered. As per

Alexander's policy if we met with resistance we were brutal. I did everything in my power to negotiate a peaceful recognition of us as conqueror. When we did have a bloodless takeover Alexander was often magnanimous even to the point of leaving the original king (caliph) in power. This often did not please our troops, for they feared rebellion from the rear. This was understandable as the last thing our aging and shrinking army needed was to be encased on all sides by enemy troops.

Looking back on it the taking of India was comparable to a modern day circuit party. If a kingdom resisted we would kill the soldiers and take the women and children as slaves. There were some truly beautiful youths brutally used by our soldiers and then put to the sword for failure to capitulate. When I could arrange a peaceful takeover the parties were magnificent with exotic foods and spices with which we were unfamiliar. Wine and liquor was supplied to us that out-ranked even the spirits we had tasted in Persia. Needless to say Alexander was drinking in epic amounts and I feared for both his health and his position.

Word had reached us from many sources that a powerful kingdom to the east was preparing for our approach. It was said their soldiers fought from the backs of enormous animals that could be as destructive as a legion of warriors. This was the powerful Nanda Empire of Magadha which not only had an enormous army but also possessed legendary wealth. These stories only whetted Alexander's appetite for battle and he used these rumors of untold wealth to inspire his men. But I wasn't so sure. The signs were not favorable. I tried to reason with Alexander saying that my astrologers (in those days all leaders would have holy men or women close at hand to foretell future events) were not optimistic and that we should wait until a future time. I emphasized that we had thirty thousand boys conscripted from the population of Persia that were trained in Macedonian warfare just waiting for our return. My advice fell often on drunken ears. The first sign that came to pass was when we faced the Aspasioi (a small but fierce Indian kingdom) and Alexander was wounded in the shoulder by a dart but eventually the Aspasioi lost the fight. We then faced the Assakenoi, who fought bravely and offered us very stubborn resistance in the strongholds of Massaga, Ora, and Aornos. The fort of Massaga could only be reduced after several days of bloody fighting in which Alexander was seriously wounded in the ankle. History has it recorded that not only did Alexander slaughter the entire population of Massaga, but he reduced its buildings to rubble. After Aornos, Alexander and I crossed the Indus and fought and won an epic battle against a local ruler Porus, who ruled a region in the Punjab, in the Battle of Hydaspes in 326 BC.

Alexander and I were greatly impressed by Porus for his bravery in battle and so we made an alliance with him, appointing him Satrap of his own kingdom; we even added land he did not own before our war with him. Of course, as with all things, this was a somewhat political gesture since controlling lands so far from Greece ultimately required assistance and the cooperation from locals. It was here that Alexander named one of the two cities he founded Bucephala, in honor of his beloved horse that had brought him to India and had died after this battle mostly from old age.

Not yet satisfied we continued east toward a destiny of sorts to the Ganges River. Frightening rumors were being filtered in from the Nanda Empire of Magadha and Gangaridai

Empire of Bengal which intimidated an already disgruntled army. Fearing the prospects of facing other powerful Indian armies and exhausted by years of campaigning our army mutinied at the Hyphasis River, refusing to march further east. And so it was that this river marked the easternmost extent of my beloved Alexander's conquests.

It seemed that the bloody struggle with Porus had blunted the Macedonian's courage. They felt that if defeating Porus, who had only been able to muster twenty thousand infantry and two thousand horses, had been such a horrendous battle, they stood little chance against the more powerful kingdoms that lay to the east. Our soldiers violently opposed us when they learned that the Ganges was a reported twenty thousand feet wide and six hundred feet deep. The rumors also had the men convinced that the kings of these empires were awaiting them with eighty thousand horsemen, two hundred thousand footmen, eight thousand chariots, and six thousand war elephants.

Alexander, seeing the unwillingness of his men eventually agreed and turned south. Along the way our army conquered the Malli clans and many other Indian tribes, whose names are best lost to history. When we began our homeward journey, I was as usual entrusted with half the army, including the elite troops and two hundred elephants, as we travelled south-west along the banks of the Hydaspes. Some of the army, including Alexander, travelled in boats, which had been supplied and sponsored by some of our newly acquired lands, who were no doubt happy to see us on our way.

It was here that Alexander made what was probably the greatest mistake of his career. He decided that we would march through the Gedrosian Desert toward home. With thousands in our convoy not to mention horses and war elephants bringing the treasures of our Asian campaign to be distributed, there simply was not enough food or water. I believe my old friend Curtius did an excellent job journaling this part of our trip.

> Their provisions exhausted, the Macedonians began to experience first the shortage of food and eventually starvation. They rummaged about for palm roots (that being the only tree growing there) but, when even this means of sustenance ran out, they began to slaughter their pack-animals, sparing not even their horses. Then, having nothing to carry their baggage, they proceeded to burn the spoils they had taken from the enemy, spoils for which they had penetrated the furthest reaches of the East.

Although, we were tortured by thirst, the army met disaster in a torrent bed, where a meager trickle of water had encouraged us to pitch camp. A sudden cloudburst over distant mountains turned the little stream into a raging flood without warning, and many of the women and children drowned. There were considerable casualties both among people and animals during the march. The sick and exhausted were left to lie where they fell; none had the strength to help or carry them. When a violent wind obliterated all landmarks and erased the tracks with sand, our guides, unable to read the stars, failed us. In this emergency, Alexander took charge personally and, using his sense of direction, led his desperate men back the sea, where a fresh-water spring was discovered under the shingle beach. Sustained by a succession of such springs, we marched along the shore for seven days. Although Alexander stood up to the hardships as well as any man, and indeed it was on this march that he displayed some of his most noble qualities, the march was an unmitigated disaster. Thousands had died. Alexander and I barely escaped, not to mention the loss of treasure and animals. Eventually an exhausted but victorious army made its way to Persia and the city of Sousa.

Alexander declared all of his soldiers heroes and rewarded every Macedonian warrior by paying off their debts and letting those who chose to return home to their wives and families with a guaranteed pension, which with the wealth we had accumulated we could well afford. After some rest and many weeks of athletic events we would begin our campaign to take all that lay west of Greece. This was to include what would become Italy and Spain and whatever lands lay to the north.

Chapter Ten
A Surprise for Hephaestion

Our lives would radically change not long after our final return to Sousa. Our strategy to return from India was working in our favor for our future expansion plans. Our thinking had a twofold purpose. First, our generals and soldiers would get to enjoy some of the enormous wealth we had acquired while conquering our world. Second, the display of their successes and the bragging rights that went with it would fire up young men from Persia to Greece as the older generation returned home as heroes. This latter would allow us to incite the youth with dreams of glory. Raising yet another invincible army to augment our thirty thousand trained Persian boys, we would take the west and return to finish what we had started in India and then to go beyond, conquering whatever worlds might be out there. We could have done it, of that I have no doubt. Alexander and I would have founded a dynasty that would have ruled the world for millennia.

How, you might wonder, would we, two men, establish a dynasty? Well, I have to admit that Alexander was one up on me there. When we had rid Persia of its flamboyant king Darius III, Alexander had the good sense to spare the life of the wife and daughters of the king. He then took not only the late king's eldest daughter Strataira but also the daughter of Darius' predecessor Artaxerxes Ochus whose name was Parysatis as his wives. At this point let me mention once again that he had taken a wife (hillbilly queen I would call her today) by the name of Roxanna. So you can imagine I was none too thrilled with this second and third wife situation, as I was concerned that it would interfere with our sex life. On that, I need not have been concerned. Politically it certainly made good sense to link himself to the old ruling royal line.

Then the unforgiveable happened. In 324 BC while we were in Susa, Alexander arranged the weddings of more than eighty Persian, Median and Bactrian aristocrats to the leading Macedonians, which included me! Unbeknownst to me, he decided I was to marry his new bride's sister, Drypetis. I could have died (actually I did four months later). You've no idea the surprise, not to mention the hurt and anger I felt when I learned of my impending nuptials. That night there were few inhabitants in the royal palace of Babylon who were not privy to my unhappiness with the god Alexander. Glasses of wine were thrown, priceless glass objects shattered, unforgiveable insults hurled by me to my king. Insults that would have cost any other man not only his life but the life of his extended family, and even his servants. Amazingly, Alexander remained somewhat passive trying every now and again to calm me down. Finally, I said something that got to him and he actually "bitch slapped" me. Well that took some nerve! But it did serve its purpose. I fell silent with only tears running down my cheeks to show my upset (I could be so dramatic).

"Hephaestion just listen to me. Let me explain my plan. I have a reason for everything I do. You know that!" Alexander pleaded.

"And what is this plan Alexander? You want to stabilize your position in Persia by making some royal bimbo your wife! That I can almost tolerate. But dragging me into it and forcing me to marry! Well that is...that is...did you see her nose? Not to mention her teeth...they would be the envy of my battle horse! On top of that I have absolutely no knowledge of what even to do with a woman! The last time I had contact with a woman there was when my body was pulled from my mother's womb." I screamed. My temper was getting out of hand again. I was always, just as I am today, the cool one, who could face an enemy king and convince him how he would benefit by forfeiting his throne to Alexander. But then Alexander always knew exactly how to push the wrong buttons with me.

"Hephaestion! Hephaestion! Please calm...now! I command it! Why so upset? You do to her what you do to me only use the other entrance. I'll have our physician diagram it for you." He laughed.

"I know that part! I'm not an idiot. It's just that I have no idea how to approach sex with a woman, what to say, how to command her to please me. I just can't rape a woman as you have been known to do."

Alexander smiled and softly said "So are you saying that is what you do to me? You know how to command me to please you? You think you are commanding the pharaoh of Egypt, the son of the god Zeus, to milk your cock so that it might please you?"

"Well....sometimes that is exactly what I do", I replied. My eyes cast downward wondering if once again I had overstepped myself.

"You are an impertinent little minx! You think you command me to please you? I am leader of the world. No, I am the world and you are just one of my subjects. You are but a man that I tolerate to live in my presence. You command me on how to please you?" Alexander hissed between clenched teeth as he confronted me within two inches of my face. Well maybe I knew how to push Alexander's buttons as well as he did mine. Suddenly I felt his right fist wrapped in an excruciating hold around my balls. At the same time his left hand had entwined itself in my hair as he forced my head down several inches and simultaneously pulled my lips to his. His tongue forcing its way into my mouth with that familiar taste I loved so much. Twenty centuries later and I still remember that taste. Pulling his lips from mine Alexander whispered almost cruelly "Tell me again how you command me to please you! That is an order from your king Hephaestion; let me hear you command me to please you!"

"My sire! It was a betrayal of my tongue uttered in anger at the thought of having to share you with yet another woman." I pleaded to no avail as his fingers tightened their viselike grip on my balls. By now his lips and teeth were on my right nipple torturing me with repeated bites. Suddenly my balls were released and both of his hands were at my nipples squeezing those erect buds each between a thumb and index finger and his mouth was once again on mine and once again I was laving the sweet nectar from his tongue. Pulling back once again "Hephaestion did I not give you a command!"

Well, what can a mere mortal do when under direct orders from a living deity? I acquiesced. "Alexander! I command you to disrobe....quickly! Now!" Bowing his head with his eyes cast shyly up to my face Alexander did as I had bid. Loosening the tie to his robe he let it slide from his shoulders and onto the ground at his feet. "Now Alexander, remove my robe." Meekly, the lord of the world removed my brocaded robe, folded it neatly and lay it down. By now the head of my cock had escaped the confines of its fleshy sheath and was upright to the point of touching just above my navel. "Bend over Alexander I want to see if a god can learn humility at the hands of a lowly man. " Alexander did as I bid and I had before me one of the most beautiful asses I have ever seen. I smiled, he not being able to see me, and then I struck with the flat of my hand and my king grunted in pain and surprise. My handprint was very evident on that beautiful chiseled ass and then another and another and still my love stayed in position. "Now Alexander, get on your knees and use that tyrant's mouth of yours to once again worship the cock of this, your most unworthy subject." Obediently, the living god took my shaft in his hand and pulled it toward his open mouth. His tongue licked the great head of my dick slowly and I could feel the buds of his tongue targeting the sensitive nerves in that pink gland. Furtive little darts of that luscious tongue tasting the steady flow of semen that, in my arousal, leaked from the slit. He knew all too well how that drives me insane and grabbing the back of his head I forced my cock down his throat until his nose was buried in my hair.

What seemed like all too short an eternity, my lover suckled my cock. As it had been since I was a boy-man Alexander's administrations were all too fast building me to my release. Gasping from the exquisite manipulation of his tongue to the underside of my prick's head I could feel the sudden tightening of my balls as my sac pulled up around them. Then started the spasms as my life seed propelled itself out of my tube and into the throat of my beloved. One shot, two, three, and on the creamy milk shot from me. I remember the feel of his hands as they tightened on the flexed globes of my ass in Alexander's effort to pull my cock further into his throat so as not to lose a drop.

As I was coming, my knees buckled and losing my balance I fell back onto Alexander's bed. It was no sooner after I felt the cool embrace of the silken covers against my back that I felt the calloused strong hands of Alexander rubbing roughly up my shins and my thighs pushing the bristling hair of my legs flat against my skin. So intense was my orgasm that it seemed that every hair follicle was an intense source of pleasure. From my supine position I looked down over my chest only to find Alexander's eyes, those great brown pools of lust, fixed on me. His mouth curled in a smile of pure sexual desire. Suddenly, I was no longer in charge of this man. Alexander had become my king and commander once more.

All signs of discipline disappeared from my warrior and I knew I would pay for my rebellion as I had many times before and too few times after. Each of Alexander's hands gripped the underside of my knees pushing my legs up and apart. "Now we will see who commands and who follows orders and what happens to anyone who disobeys me," Alexander stated slowly and way too softly. The smile was still there and I thought I noticed the pink of his tongue flicking from between those ivory white too perfectly even teeth and dance across his upper lip.

Just as suddenly his face disappeared between my thighs. I felt his nose pushing up my ball sac and without subtleties his tongue plunged into that place with which he was so familiar. I had just come down from orgasm and now every nerve about that aperture was being assaulted by Alexander's oral muscle. By now all I was aware of was the grip of his hands on the top of each of my tensed thighs and the tickling caused by those beautiful curled locks of his golden blonde hair as they rubbed the tip of my rehardening dick. As I groaned louder and louder on my journey back to submission I couldn't help but note the eyes of Xylop, Alexander's manservant watching us from his position near the chamber door, I knew my warrior king of kings was preparing me for complete invasion and total occupation.

Positioning me and himself on the bed Alexander raised my

ankles to his shoulders. He was upright on his knees. "Xylop! Bring the honey oil here." Immediately, Xylop fetched a precious glass bottle beside a great marble tub near a balcony overlooking Babylon and brought it to his king. "Don't just stand there slave! Pour the oil into your hands and lather my cock in it." Obediently the manservant laved the precious sweet oil on Alexander's massive veined penis, pushing the foreskin off the sensitive head. "Now rub the ointment on this insolent Chiliarch's hole. Then I want you to put some in your mouth and force the oil in his canal. I'm going to show him mercy and make my entry as pleasant as possible." Alexander stated with a leering grin on his face. As bidden, Xylop filled his mouth with the honey oil and laying his head to the side beneath the kneeling Alexander with his face toward my ass. I could feel his lips form a seal at my anus and his tongue teasing me open so he could force his mouth load of oil into my hungry orifice.

"Tell me you regret your words and actions against your king and perhaps I will not force this humiliation upon you! Perhaps I will even spare your life," Alexander oozed the last words out slowly in his most imperial tone. I just lay there, ankles on his shoulders and my eyes looking into his as defiantly as I could.

"I said tell me...ask my forgiveness and as surely as I am the son of Zeus I will get up from here and let you walk away not only with your life but with your pride." Alexander was a master of the dramatic.

"Why, in the name of the gods, would I beg for the forgiveness and mercy of a little king who, under my ministrations, I have heard squeal like the women being fucked by your soldiers? I think not! You are but a parchment tiger. Now, get up and I will leave your presence and your reputation intact and the world need not know you must have an army to back up the smallest of threats," this last I said emphasizing the word "smallest of threats" and eyeing his erect cock. All of this was being overheard and observed by Xylop. Was that a smile that quickly passed over the slave's face?

These last words seemed to be the catalyst. Alexander's eyes had formed wide wild circles. There was that familiar look of madness he always had before charging into battle, his temples moved in distinct twitches. I was always able to cause a plethora of ticks in my beloved. As if in slow motion his mouth opened wide and a scream of absolute rage filled the room. "Then expect no mercy!" Those were the last words I heard before I felt the massive knob of Alexander's great unsheathed and unguided cock assault and successfully penetrate my canal, completing filling me until all nine inches were in me. The pain was beyond words as I agonized with that incredibly intense burning that I loved so much! Not for one second was I given opportunity to get acclimated to girth and depth of his dick before he had pulled back eight inches and just as quickly thrust back in to full depth. I had gotten what I was after! This went on thrust after thrust with the ecstasy taking over almost immediately. Of course I didn't show the pleasure, I had to go along with the "punishment" and besides, I had invested too much time getting this fuck to act like I was enjoying it. The crown of Alexander's cock and the curve of his shaft were perfect for the stimulation of my P-spot. My love, you see, had been designed by the gods just for my pleasure.

For fifteen minutes my punishment went on before Alexander, now somewhat winded and dripping in sweat rasped "Are you sorry for saying those things to me?"

Well, I'm not completely without heart "You know I always am. As you tell me I share your soul and as such your temperament. When I get out of hand it is only you who can bring me under control." For good measure I wept this last into his ear. "Please just forgive me like you always do and make love to me as you did long ago in your palace in Macedon, before the world was ours and we thought only of each other's pleasure." On this last plead I was being quite honest. It has always been good for me (and I daresay anyone reading this) to go into the mind and dwell in the pleasures of things past.

"Why did you get so angry?" Alexander whispered into my ear, moving that great cock of his ever so slightly against my inside pleasure spot. I grunted and then explained. You see it was always easier to explain things that I disagreed with Alexander on after a great fight and vigorous fuck.

"Everything is happening so fast! We have conquered the world only to find that there will be more worlds unknown to conquer. There appears to be no time for us ever. Then you marry the daughter of Darius and that other woman after just marrying that tedious Roxanne four years ago. Then without my knowledge or approval I find myself the husband to be of Stateira's sister. All of this and then there is the issue of the dead king's eunuch, Bagoas. You fuck him almost as much as you do me. He is truly more beautiful than me and with none of the scars of battle on his perfect body. In truth Alexander I am jealous of all this and I truly wonder where I will fit in with your future. What I am saying is that I have my doubts that you are creating our future and feel more you are designing just your future as you carve this new world of yours."

Another slight withdrawal of his cock and we both grunted in unison as he moved it back in me to its full depth, he locked his gaze on my eyes lowered his head toward me and lovingly nipped at my lower lip before speaking. "Hephaestion, how can you even begin to question any of my actions? Since we were but boys every plan I have ever made has included you, excepting none. I have explained my marriage to the princess Straetira and you agreed that it made good diplomatic sense to link myself with the deposed ruling family in order to kindle allegiance of the people and it seems to be working. I think you know me well enough to know that I have no interest in her other than that and to provide me with an heir. Once pregnant I will never touch her again. In fact if you had any inclination that way I would let you father a child with her and that would satisfy me as to my heir. Remember when the king's widow and daughters were brought before us after we had lay claim to Babylon? When the old queen mistook you for me and was begging for the lives of her daughters that even when she was made aware of her error I spoke up telling her in front of all my men not to worry about the mistake for in truth you are also Alexander. I meant that then and I will always feel that way.

My hope is that you will father a child with my wife's sister and that our great grandchildren, far removed cousins by then, will marry and our bloodlines will truly be joined and our descendants will rule the world forever." Alexander emphasized this last with another slight withdrawal and reinsertion of that beautiful thick dick.

"But what of this eunuch, Bagoas?" I asked. Liking his first explanation I had to see if he could carry this one through to my satisfaction.

"Bagoas is truly beautiful as you said but in my eyes not more so than you. I do have feelings for him, but as a possession not as an equal, certainly. He is neither man nor woman. He is a conquered slave. I must say he intrigues me with his knowledge in the art of lovemaking. It is a Persian thing. I understand why Darius had him as a prized possession. You know that I would gladly share him with you if you were willing to do it. But of one thing you can be certain no man alive, dead, or yet to be born has been given the permission to fuck me except you. You know that! The only way my ass will feel the invasion of another man's cock besides yours is if it is done to my body after I have been laid waste by death." Alexander finished all of this never taking his gaze from me and I knew in my heart, as I actually had before the fight, that he was speaking with total fidelity.

"I believe you Alexander. Why do you always start these fights with me?" I asked. But before he could protest, I smiled kissed his lips and opened my mouth so that I could allow entry of his tongue. A quick look of exasperation and he made several long and very deep thrusts in me. I could feel the swell of his already massive pole, the tightening of his thighs between mine and the gush of his essence filling me.

After the servant had washed both of us and rubbed in exotic oil, we retired to Alexander's bed for what was left of the night. With the silken sheets laying lightly over us Alexander on his left side pulled me into a cuddling position with me also lying on my left side. As was our custom when not in a battle encampment, we slept nude the hair on the front of his thighs pushing the hair on the back of my thighs. Kissing me gently on the back of my neck Alexander placed his right hand on my knee and pulled my leg up. This had happened many times in the past. I could feel the oil covered cock of my king as its blunt crown penetrated me slowly and deeply once more that night. My knee fell back into place against my left leg and Alexander's right arm lay against my chest. Subtle little movements followed while he kissed my neck...a quickening, a soft sound of release into me. And then we slept with him filling me. I don't remember being aware of when he slipped out of me. I wish I could remember. It is sad that we take usual occurrences for granted as if it will always be like this. But it's not. This was to be the last time that we were to sleep this way.

Chapter Eleven
The Dark Gift

My death came over a several day period. History suspects cholera. Some historians conjecture that I was poisoned. In fact, aside from actually having a fever, I was being changed from what I was then to what I am now, an immortal in the guise of a vampire. So many of your vampire writers from the last century and even into this new millennium repeatedly indicate that the vampire looks upon his or her condition as a curse, as an affliction thrust upon them against their will. Not so for me. Certainly I was not looking for my gift but I would be less than truthful if I said the last twenty-three centuries has not been a hell of a ride!

There was excitement everywhere as the time of the games approached. Both Alexander and I were excellent athletes, even at our ripe age of thirty-two. Weeks of planning were about to come to fruition. This time Alexander and I were not going to be participants but proud observers of the youth that made up the teams. There would be much partying, festive dinners, dancers both female and eunuch providing entertainment when there were no competitions being performed. I had gotten so that anymore I was apprehensive about the partying. Alexander had, over the past couple of years, as I have repeatedly stated, begun to drink strong wine more and more. This often was to his detriment. It was one thing for a youth to drink to drunkenness in celebration but to drink to alleviate stress was another matter. My king had gotten to where even a small amount of alcohol would cloud his judgment and he would publicly make a fool of himself to no good end. It was on such an occasion that he had killed a loyal friend out of anger. It was no small amount of time that I spent repairing that blunder. I had sickened of watching his hands shake for half the day as he recovered from the previous night's indulgence. I had my suspicions that both his wife and the eunuch Pagoas intentionally encouraged drinking as a way of getting him to do as they wanted. There were even times that I could not reason with him.

So it was in the spring of 324 BC I left Susa where I had been married, and accompanied Alexander and the rest of the army to Ecbatana. Having made it a leisurely trip, conquering a few opposing clans along the way, we arrived in the autumn just before the start of the games and festivals. At the beginning of our second day there, I started feeling quite nauseous after I got up and by late afternoon had a very high fever and muscle aches to the point that I could not stand and walk without assistance. Alexander was summoned and came to my chamber. At first he joked that perhaps at long last the gods had answered his prayers to make me with child, but he quickly knew that this was serious. He sat by my bed throughout the evening foregoing dinner since the smell of food was overpowering for me. I was beginning to drift in and out of consciousness and he kept his lips close to my ears whispering all the time how I would be ok and would be able to join him at the games within days. Then he began saying that he would not go to the events without me. I was aware enough to catch that and insisted he go especially after the comment of one of his generals had been making the rounds that the world and "Alexander is ruled by Hephaestion's thighs." While there is some truth in that, I didn't want to give it any foundation. At length he agreed and left me with his physician, Glaucias issuing to him strict orders to heal me. Poor physician, I was to be his last patient.

My condition worsened over the next couple of days. The poor physician did everything he knew to do, and some things he did not, to bring back my health. At some point a healer from the desert mountains by the name of Xaphaxes called on my doctor assuring him that he had the means to heal me and that from the story he was hearing of my symptoms I was suffering from an ailment well know to his people. At his wits end and forgoing the customary screening he was given permission to attend me.

Xaphaxes brought me ointments and a foul tasting broth to drink. He said magical words over me all the while waving his hands in dramatic gestures. I had an immediate foreboding of this man dressed in old style Persian garb with his neck weighted down in rare gems and golden strands. He had a long beard tightly curled like the ancient Persian carvings found at some of the ruins of this ancient country. His Persian was of an accent with which I was unfamiliar and some of his words had no meaning to me or my attendants. The strange thing was that I was beginning to feel better. The hallucinations of fever had left me within minutes of drinking this foul tasting broth he had kept forcing past my lips. My own physician's countenance was one of obvious relief and no doubt he was preparing to take credit for my recovery.

The night of the fourth day of my illness became one of enlightenment for me. Xaphaxes had convinced my doctor that I should be left alone with him and even my guards and servants should be out of my chamber as he had to chant magical words over my body to make the healing complete. He insisted that no man should hear these words as they had been given to him by one of the great healing gods of Persia with a promise of utmost secrecy or all who heard them would die. My physician being a man who did not like taking chances with the old gods agreed with Xaphaxes and my servants and guards were dismissed to an antechamber within my call should I have need of assistance.

I still can remember my room that night. There was a table

with bottles of precious oils over its entire surface and a wide doorway leading to a balcony that overlooked the city of Ecbatana. The moon was at its fullest and gave way to a beautiful view of the great temple of Ishtar with hundreds of torches burning on every tier. My walls were covered in brocaded linens the like of which can no longer be produced. The mattress on which I lay was three feet thick and filled with feathers that had each had their hard quills removed. It was like sleeping on a dream I can remember thinking....so different from the cots with stretched skins that had supported me and Alexander during years of campaigning and late night fucking. I must confess that a feather mattress in a palace or a cot on a battlefield served equally well for long bouts of coitus but then so did a table or a chair when one is properly leaned over it. I really miss those days.

Releasing thoughts of some good times and coming back to the present I was aware of Xaphaxes standing over me and looking down at me. This went on for the longest time it seems to me. Finally just wanting him to do his thing and get out of my room I asked him, "When are you going to do whatever you need to do to cure me and to speed your departure from my chamber?" I realize this did not sound appreciative in that I really was feeling better, but I had an intense distrust for this man. For no reason that I could pinpoint he just made me uneasy.

"Unfortunately, Hephaestion, I cannot heal you because I don't know how. That is I cannot heal you in the way you want or expect." He said this almost sadly. Naturally, being an inquisitive young man I asked him what the fuck (the actual translation is difficult) that was supposed to mean.

"Let me tell you a story. I will make it as brief as possible as I don't think you have that much time." Again, I'm thinking what the fuck does he mean by that? I was feeling four hundred per cent better after all.

"You will recall the ruins you and your army passed through four days ride to the east of Babylon?" he continued dismissing my look of impatience. I nodded; I could remember a vast field of weathered marble. While it was possible to tell that a city had once stood there barely one stone still lay on top of another. Here and there the remnants of steps could be depicted among the occasional column. Alexander and I were curious about what people had lived here. When we had questioned nomads in the area about this deserted place we found that it was so old that even these superstitious people had no knowledge of its beginnings. The ruins had been vast enough to become our dinner topic that night but except for a note jotted down by our historian it had quickly lost our interest as words of a new rebellion had reached us.

Xaphaxes proceeded, "Four thousand years ago that was a city that rivaled today's Babylon in grandeur. While your ancestors fought among themselves just to maintain simple wooden encampments, the people of Barure were drinking the finest wine and building monoliths to the gods. I don't even know how old our civilization really was. We had accumulated untold wealth over the centuries. Most of what we knew is now lost. The lands around Barure were fertile with a great river that fed our economic life. Of course there is no river now or even a trace of one.

The citizens were ruled by an absolute monarch but a benevolent one. There were problems of course. It was a constant struggle to keep marauders out and, unfortunately, we had to support slavery to keep vast building campaigns going. But there were laws to protect even them and after service to our country they were granted freedom, citizenship and a piece of land. While there may have been some inequities it was overall a good place to spend one's life. Then a force that even our gods could not protect us from descended up Barure. It was the illness that infects you and that will kill you before another day is past. That is unless you accept the gift I can give you just as I accepted it over four thousand years ago."

Now, of course, I'm thinking this man is even sicker than I am. What kind of delusional idiot have they left me with anyway? But I just lay there looking up at that strange man, my eyes unable to leave his gaze and for some reason my voice was not mine to cry out for security.

"The sickness was swift. Our temple fires smoked from the burning of sacred incense by our priests but the gods did not answer our prayers for deliverance. When there were no holy men left to present our petitions, panic ensued and the citizens began to flee the city, most only to perish. There were some survivors, perhaps one in a hundred who did not catch the illness. But with the army decimated, religious and educational leaders gone, and government ended they became wanderers. Most probably died at the hands of unfriendly neighboring states, others probably became slaves, and I like to think that some blended in to other civilizations and that their blood lives on somewhere today. I may never know the answer to that."

"What about you? How did you survive?" I found myself buying into his story. Something in my gut told me that he was telling me the truth or at least that he believed what he was telling me.

"I didn't really, but I am coming to that. Just listen for now to what I have to say. Our time together is growing short. You must hear me and make a decision. I will abide by whatever you say. If you decide you want what I offer I will give you the gift and spend some time instructing you on what you will need to know. If you decide you do not want it then I will leave you here to die naturally. Either way that you decide no one will remember that I was ever here." Xaphaxes stated this to me calmly and without apparent malice.

"You have my permission to continue." I told him. I noted that his expression betrayed some amusement at my giving him permission.

"I found myself lying in my bed chamber burning with the fever. I had retched to the point that my stomach acids burned my throat. I was yelling for water. At first I was demanding it but after a while I found myself pleading for someone to bring me water. I did not realize then that there was no one in my house to bring me anything. For the first time in my life I was alone. It occurred to me that I was going to die there in my great bed and that I would not have benefit of proper entombment. I almost found it humorous that the great monument that had taken thirty years to build and could be seen from miles away would remain empty, except for perhaps the occasional nomad and of course opportunistic vermin. I felt that the gods, unhappy with some action on my part, had sentenced me, King Xaphaxes to rot where I died." He said this as he looked out the window at the flickering torches of the distant temple.

"King Xaphaxes!" I said incredulous that this man's position outranked my own.

"Yes Hephaestion. It is strange isn't it, that I found myself king of a people who had either died or fled? Then he went on with his saga. "I lay there for perhaps another full day so sick and thirsty that I prayed for death to take me. I no longer worried about what would happen to my Ka as the Egyptians referred to the conscious. Then on the last sunset of my life I opened my eyes. Standing by my bed were two men dressed in robes of purple and white. These men were strangers of that I was certain. Just as you and Alexander, one had black hair and the other gold. Both had long tresses that hung over their shoulders. Their skin was quite pale. They were truly beautiful, with eyes the color of which I had never seen. When the light hit their eyes from one direction they were like pools of blue sapphire but with the slightest movement of the head they sparkled with a deep emerald green. The thought flashed through my fevered mind, that if these men were not gods, then the gods must have sent them to me so I could die amidst beauty. During my life I had genuinely loved women and men. As sick as I was I wondered what it would be like to spend a hedonistic night with these two. Then I came back to the reality of the situation. Perhaps these two young men were from an enemy state and had wondered into my palace intent upon killing me. If that were so I wished that they would do it quickly. As if reading my mind, they turned to each other and then looked down at me with a smile. They assured me that they meant no harm to me and in fact had come to offer a gift. They explained that unlike you Hephaestion, I only had minutes to live, not a few hours. They told me what I have told you. It was not in their power to save my life but that they could give me a death that if I used it right could be more fulfilling than my life had ever been. They explained that they were the immortal descendents of a race so ancient that they didn't even know its origins. For eons they had simply watched the progressions and regressions of human kind. Once or twice in a five hundred year period they would leave their habitat and offer this gift, which they called the 'dark gift,' to certain members of mankind whom they felt could contribute."

"Why call it the 'dark gift,' if it is an honor to be given it?" I asked, even more mesmerized by this tale.

"Ahh, I asked the same question Hephaestion." The ancient king told me. "They told me that it was in many ways truly a 'dark gift.' Because it meant that the receiver must give up all with which he was familiar. His family, his home, his position, all that he loves can no longer be a part of his existence. I would be a member of a very secret society whose existence must be hidden from a barbaric world. Also to consider was the fact that grief could be overwhelming as we watched the people we love and the society that we cherished grow old, wither, and turn to dust while we do not change. They told me that would not be a problem for me since everyone I loved and knew was gone already. Also the gift is dark to those who cherish life, for we must sometimes take life especially at first. You see we must drink the blood of the living. Sometimes, actually more often than not, we kill our food supply simply because we are a novice. Do we feel guilt at first? Yes, or at least if we have chosen the fledgling correctly there should be some remorse. The key is to seek out your life source with educated discretion, but that takes a while. Eventually you will learn to feed mainly on only those who society will not miss or those whose light is fired by the pain of others. But at all times you must remember never to act in such a way that the world suspects our being among them. Because of that many human monsters must be allowed to live. The best our kind can do is to incite change, not force it.

It was about then that I realized these creatures were

speaking to me in unison but without sound. They were actually speaking in my mind. Just, Hephaestion, as I now am speaking to you." I realized at that moment that his lips were not moving and yet I was hearing his story. When he had started this form of communication I was not clear, but communicating he was.

His thoughts continued. "They then told me I had been a beneficent king who loathed the concept of slavery and the barbarism of war. They felt that had I lived I would eventually have ended this yoke of human bondage, but because of the pestilence they wouldn't know for sure. What they felt certain was that if I joined them my works could continue in different ways. Once more they asked me if I would choose the true death or a death that embraces life. I was informed that I had less than five minutes time to decide for after that I would possibly be in other hands and beyond even their ability to help. It was all happening too fast. I had spent much of my time as a monarch weighing my options carefully before making a decree. I felt the nausea and dizziness consuming me again. I could feel the blackness begin to engulf me. Just as I lost consciousness I remember saying 'I choose you!'

When next I awakened I found myself no longer in Barure. I was in what must have been the land of the men who had been in my room. My new surroundings were bright and my bed comfortable, but much more simple than I was used to as king. Physically I had never felt so complete. The illness was gone with no traces I could feel remaining. When I arose from my bed and walked to the door there was lightness to my step that I had never felt before. I noticed a reflection glass on one of the walls. Walking over to it I saw myself or what I thought must be myself. I was still me but the lines that leadership had etched into my face were gone. By every appearance I was the handsome young prince that had ascended the throne forty years before. Later I was to learn that our appearance can present itself in many ways. For most of us we see ourselves as we were when we were most happy or trouble free in life. That is also how others perceive us. When I came here as a healer, I presented a believable image.

It was not long before I was joined by the young men who had brought me here. I was to learn that the dark haired one was Anak and the golden one was Maneti.

My lessons began immediately. I was told all that was known about this ancient race in which I had just become its newest member. I was told about what was happening in the world around me and about cultures that I had never heard of before. I learned many things of which humankind will not be privy to for a hundred generations and possibly longer. I found that my mind was quicker than it had ever been in life. I was like a sea sponge, absorbing everything introduced to me. So many things became clear and concepts that had been such a mystery to me in life were so simple. I was introduced to other members of this society in which I found myself. Some spent their time mainly in groups simply thinking while others I learned had the power to tap into the minds of individual humans and study them wherever in the world they were. In doing this they could predict events. No, Hephaestion, they were not seers nor could or can they tell the future with absolute certainty, but experience has given them the ability to profile possible occurrences from the actions of individuals and even whole societies with some accuracy. I was told that this race of men was called Quermen. So I was now a Quermen too.

The hardest part for me was the hunger that would happen every forty eight hours. That was as close as I felt to pain and yet it was not pain. It was more of a longing for something that I knew I had to have. It was a feel of something missing something that placed me on the edge of discomfort. Initially my two mentors gave me goblets of what I knew was dark red blood. I didn't even ask its source. I simply drank it down with relish and instant relief. The feeling that it provided was warmth that sent jolts of light to my every fiber. It was not many days before I felt the burning in the roof of my mouth. The 'dark gift' was providing a way for me to procure my own food just like the young of any species. My fangs were breaking through. Incredibly sharp they were retractable and would appear at will or when I had gone too long between feeding.

When the time was right Anak and Maneti escorted me through what seemed like endless passages to what looked like a rock wall. We simply walked through it as if it wasn't there. (I now believe that somehow we can walk through the infinitesimally small spaces between the atoms of a solid). I found that the Habitat, as it was called, was a vast compound created inside of an enormous mountain. It is likely that it will never be discovered. I have no idea how long I had been sequestered in the mountain Habitat when I finally walked out of the rock with my two friends. It was night and I knew it was cold but I didn't feel any discomfort. I also need to mention that the three of us were totally unclothed. In the Habitat clothing really wasn't necessary and I had not seen a being there that would have reason to hide anything. My escorts taught me the concept of speed and how to use our mind to lock on to human thought. In a matter of seconds I could hear in my mind the hum of hate and impending death. Maneti acknowledged my discovery by a nod and taking my hand we went faster than sound to a small encampment of rowdy soldiers who were in the process of taking turns raping four young men one at a time.

We remained out of sight of the warriors as we witnessed a short squat soldier pulling his fat stubby cock from the bloody asshole of an unfortunate young man being held bent over a rock and held in place by three soldiers. It was evident the rapist had just ejaculated in the youth as the man grunted in drunken satisfaction whipped his knife from the sheath tied to his waist and slit the boy's throat. I could hear the blood splattering against the leather vests of the two soldiers holding the boy's arms and I could even feel the agony of the youth who screamed a silent plea in his mind. The men carelessly rolled the limp body off the rock and it hit the ground with a dull thud. Another soldier assumed the previous killer's place, pulling his cock free of its confining cloth, as another boy was brought and placed on the rock. The perpetrator ripped the boy's loincloth from his body.

'There is your meal,' Maneti stated to me simply indicating the soldier who was preparing to ram his pole into the luckless boy. 'This is your first so we are going to help you. Eventually you will develop your own feeding style, but for now follow my lead.' That said Maneti walked out of the shadows followed closely by Anak and myself.

'Let the boy go.' Maneti ordered the soldiers, who looked at us in amazement. I could feel their confusion as they were approached by three tall nude unarmed men and one of them with golden hair, which I could tell they had never seen before. In fact, they had never seen any men like us before. Likewise, I had not encountered such beings as them either. I could mentally hear them take note of our height and especially our large round eyes and the pale skin of my two companions. In comparison their eyes were oblong slits and their skin had a yellow appearance not bronze like my own and all were quite short. The soldier whose turn it was to commit the rape had swung around to see who was speaking to them. I noted that he had generously applied the dead boy's blood to his cock as a form of lubrication. I felt true rage for the first time ever.

Their soldier's training quickly replaced their initial surprise as each withdrew swords from scabbards suspended from their belts. I felt them realize that we had no fear of them as we continued walking toward them. 'Follow your instincts Xaphaxes.' Was all that Maneti counseled me. In the blink of an eye I was at the rapist's side. It was a quick an uncomplicated business. I grabbed his greasy hair by my fist and pulling his head back, which made his neck quite taunt, I sank my teeth into the throbbing vein in his neck and drank deeply and long. As I drank his life's fluid I saw every killing this man had ever done. I saw that he and his comrades were rogue soldiers who fought not as patriots for their country but used their uniform for random acts of the most unspeakable violence; the murder and ravishment of innocents. My cohorts had done much the same as I. I knew from my lessons at the Habitat that the enlightened and ancient Quermen often went for many centuries without feeding and felt no ill effects. But I understood that these soldiers were despicable enough for Maneti and Anak to make exception. I quit drinking my victim's blood before he was dead and immediately launched myself on the fourth rogue who was running into the darkness. I drank a little from him before breaking his legs and leaving him there on the ground with bone sticking from his flesh below the knee. I then returned to the encampment. During this time the remaining village boys cowered together fearing that their fates may have taken a turn for the worse, as if that were possible.

We learned that the boys had been walking from a religious ceremony back to their own small village when the four soldiers had found and taken them. There had been eight of them, but the rogues had raped and killed the others the previous night. We gave them some of the soldier's provisions, told them not to stop walking until they were in the safety of their village. We were going to make them forget us but decided against it. They were still thanking us as they disappeared into the darkness. The four soldiers still lay around us. Three of them were weak from blood loss and the fourth, which we had witnessed, killing the boy, lay in agony with his broken legs. Without speaking we drove four large wooden poles, we had conveniently found, deeply into the ground. Apparently my two teachers liked what I had done to the fourth soldier and all had their legs broken. In a form of symbolic punishment we impaled each of their filthy arseholes on a pole and left them there to make their peace with whatever they might have believed. 'Sometimes violence is the only response that fits a crime' "is all that Anak thought to me.

I returned with my two friends to the compound and satiated, the three of us made love together. It was the first time since my death that I had experienced lovemaking as a Quermen and while that is a private matter I don't wish to share with you Hephaestion, it was beyond description. After the first few times of assisting me to feed, my instructors started letting me go on my own.

Not much after that I was brought before a council, for lack of a better term, where I was told they felt the choice to turn me Quermen had been wise. I must now make a decision as to what I wanted to do with my immortality. Did I desire to go out into the world among men and try to be of benefit to mankind or would I prefer to remain mostly in the Habitat. My decision came quickly to me. I wanted to remain in the Habitat where Anak and Maneti had invited me to be a threesome with them. In so doing I could use my time listening to humans hoping to find some who would have the potential to make a positive difference in a barbaric world.

I have now told you my story in its briefest form Hephaestion, because your time grows shorter and shorter. What will you decide?" Xaphaxes asked.

"I hope you decide to become Quermen with us. We believe you could make a difference to mankind." This had come from a corner of the room that I was not able to see. Suddenly two stunning men were standing next to Xaphaxes. There was no need for an introduction.

"Decide quickly Hephaestion. What do you want?" The one I knew to be Anak asked.

I was very confused. This was happening much too fast. Just one a week ago I had been riding beside Alexander laughing and talking about the games and the parties we would give in honor of the victors. Now I lay here sicker than I had ever been and was being told by what might be imaginary spirits or a dream that I had minutes to live. I must seek Alexander's opinion. I must know what he wants me to do.

"Alexander will not be here in time for you. Even if he was he would have no advice to give you. His only thought would be concern that you are out of your mind from the fever." Maneti stated.

I knew what they said was true. Alexander was an hour's ride away, so at best it would be two hours before he could be here considering it would take a full hour for my summons to reach him. The nausea was creeping back in accompanied by stomach pain and dizziness. I knew I was drifting in and out of awareness, but each time I felt awake my three visitors were standing by my bed watching me with what I took to be compassion and waiting for my answer.

"Hephaestion, your heartbeat has slowed and it labors to push your thickening blood through your body. Your doctor and servants have grown concerned that something is amiss. We must have your answer in the next minute or you will be lost to wherever the true death takes you." King Xaphaxes warned me.

The reality hit me and fear, something I had never felt in my thirty-two years took over. "I want to live! Help me please!" I pleaded.

Very quickly one of the men, I believe it was Anak, gave me a mindplant, explaining very quickly what to expect and what I would feel over the next few days. My body would be dead by all accounts but I would remain aware of what was happening around me. When the time was right the three of them would take me with no one in the world being the wiser. The Quermen advised that they would communicate with me and walk me through the process until the time of my body's resurrection. I now understood...at least some of it. Rapidly each of the three Quermen (vampires you now call their kind) punctured the palm of their hand and each in turn placed it over my mouth. I was told to drink. I sucked the metallic tasting blood from each until each had told me to stop. I thought I would retch from the unfamiliar taste but I did not. Then Xaphaxes bent over me. At first he lightly kissed my lips (had I not been so weak I would have protested fearing I had foul breath) and then he gently turned my head to its side. From the corner of my eyes I could see his mouth open and I saw two sharp fangs descend from behind his canine teeth (how white they are I thought) and he lowered his mouth against my neck. There was a slight sting from penetrating my skin. I was expecting that he would suck my blood as he had described doing during a feed, but he didn't. Instead I felt numbness and then blackness enveloped me. Later I learned that much like a snake the fangs of Quermen are hollow and can inject venom like substance that aids in the transition from mortal to immortal.

I don't know how long I dwelt in the depths of darkness but it must not have been long. For the next thing I was aware of was the shouting. Some of the voices I recognized as those of my servants and certainly I knew the panic stricken voice of Glaucias, Alexander's physician.

"What do you mean he was in here alone? For how long was he alone?" screamed the hysterical doctor. "Fetch Alexander at once and tell him to spare no time." And as an afterthought I heard Glaucias yell to the departing men "If you value your life you will not tell the Shahanshah that we found him alone ….and dead!"

So I really was dead or at least I appeared to have been pronounced so by poor Glaucias. There was much movement in my room. I felt hands with wet rags washing my body of the smell of sickness. My eyes remained opened but I could not blink and yet I could see anything that got in my line of sight.

In moments I heard a deep voice. "What has happened to him? Is he alright?" The rich timbre came from Aristenes. There was silence from all in the room. Then I heard people moving aside as rapid footsteps made their way to my bedside. There was my beautiful young ward standing over me, a look of complete shock on his face. Of course! He would not even have known I was sick. He had remained behind in Sousa to complete some important assignments I had given him. I had given orders for a score of soldiers to safely escort him to Ecbatana as soon as his duties were complete. Alexander and I were looking forward to his joining us. We had even discussed adopting him into our family and giving him royal title of prince. We had agreed that a royal title would be beneficial for the diplomatic duties I had planned for him. All of that was a mute now. Suddenly the youth knelt beside my bed and began kissing my face and pleading with the gods to bring me back. Then he raised his face from mine and those bottomless orbs stared into my unmoving dead eyes. The realness of the situation seemed to take over as his countenance changed to gentle intelligence. He knew I was gone. His soft manly hands kept stroking my face as he looked at me. I could feel his tears dropping onto my face.

"This cannot be," he whispered as if to me. "What will Alexander do without Hephaestion? The world will surely plunge into darkness. Oh! What will Alexander do without him?" I had been right about Aristenes. His grief was not for himself but for Alexander. His intelligence told him that I was beyond being helped and that his concerns had to be for the living. My mind screamed at the depth of pain this boy was feeling at losing me and I cried inwardly knowing that he would hide those feelings out of respect for Alexander. Still he kneeled there and continued stroking my pale face, a sob silently wracking his shoulders every few seconds. Suddenly I saw hands come from behind him and pulling him back. It was Dr. Glaucias.

"Get the boy out of here for his own sake. He should not be in this room when Alexander gets here. In fact it would be nice if none of us had to be here. It might be better to get him out of the palace altogether. It is hard to say who Alexander will take this out on." Glaucias was right. I didn't know how Alexander would react either. To my knowledge he had never lost any one he truly loved. Everybody loved Aristenes and I was touched by their genuine consideration for him. Aristenes protested saying he wanted to be with Alexander but finally he was reasonable and let them lead him out when an officer convinced him that I would want him to be safe and that Alexander would need him later.

Chapter Twelve
Alexander Surrenders to Grief

It could not have more than an hour when I saw Alexander standing above me looking down with complete disbelief at my now cooling and very pale face. He leaned down and kissed me full upon the lips ordering me to quit joking with him. This was not a funny thing to do and I had interrupted his games he spoke in a confused way that I had never heard from him before. Then he was silent and I saw the rage come into his red watering eyes.

"How could this have happened? Where is Glaucias? I gave him orders to make Hephaestion well!" Alexander had stood and looked around the room. He spotted the physician who had his arms spread out in a vain attempt to appeal his situation.

"My king, the Chiliarch was much better. He drank his broth and indicated he wanted to sleep and be left alone. We did as he commanded us to do. But against my advice he had a large amount of boiled fowl brought to him and I am told he drank a large cooler of wine. That is what killed him of that I would wager my life." The physician pled to the king. Well, this was all news to me, but then the truth would not have sounded any better. I could understand the old doctor not telling Alexander that an old man in ancient Persian dress had come to the palace claiming to be a healer and had, at the healer's request, been left alone with the man he loved. I actually felt sorry for the respected physician that had travelled with Alexander for these many years. I knew that Xaphaxes had charmed his way in with a mindplant. The ancient king had people see him as an aged mystic healer not as his youngish handsome self. It was understandable that Glaucias and none of the servants recalled the strange man's visit or why they had left him in the room alone.

Alexander was over my face again and once more kissed my lips. I was still able to feel his touch, which was moist with tears. As much as I loved him and well as I knew him, I was surprised that his beautiful face could show such utter sadness. Then I saw once more the rage coming back into his eyes. All compassion and understanding was gone and I could see a spark of madness.

"You lie to me Glaucias! How dare you blame his death on him? Were you mad to take the orders of a fevered man to leave him alone? I ask that of anyone in this room. How dare any of you leave his side? You say he ordered and consumed a large breakfast of fowl and quenched his thirst with a large cooler of wine?" The physician affirmed this question with a nod of his head. "Glaucias, Hephaestion was repulsed by the thought of wine early in the day. I say to you that you are a liar old healer! By your own wager Glaucias you bet your life that he died for disobeying your orders and not only eating but drinking wine as well. I take you up on your wager and I tell you now you have lost." Raged the king at the terrified physician. I could see his back and head shaking in fury. "I would kill you myself with my sword, which has silenced a thousand men, but your blood would soil my blade." Alexander turned back to me and looking down at my body one more time; he swung back around, his face toward Glaucias.

"Craeterus escort him out and execute him before the sun sets." Ordered the young Shahanshah to his general, who had returned from the games with him. Then in a lower voice, almost as an afterthought Alexander gave further instructions to Craeterus. "Find out the names of all who were supposed to be attending to the Chiliarch's care this morning. They must die with the doctor. Hold back cremation and instead bury them without their names being spoken or inscribed so that their souls may wander Hades forever." This was a worse sentence than death, to be nameless and lost. I could hear the wails of the poor souls being escorted from my chambers. If I could have stopped this I would have.

When the soldiers had taken the condemned out, Alexander ordered all of those remaining to leave. It was just my lover and me in the room now. He stood looking at me audibly sobbing, not caring who might be outside the chamber listening. Kneeling by my bed he looked down at me yet again staring, his eyes as unblinking as my own. I felt his salty tears falling into my dry eyes. 'If only I could console you.' I thought in vain.

"Hephaestion, why have you left me alone in this world? Everything I have done I have done for you. It is all without meaning now. I have no one to share it with. Many people love the king Alexander, but in the entire world you are the only one who loved Alexander." With those words he kissed me again and then gently closed my eyes. I could no longer see what was going on but I knew, as if through some sense I had never possessed before.

I heard Alexander stand and the sound of his dropping belt with its sword hit the ground. I recognized the sound of his leg leathers being removed. I wasn't sure why. In recent times I would have recognized those sounds as a sign that his naked body was going to slide in next to mine.

"Hephaestion, I am going to lie next to you as I have thousands of times before. I want to hold you gently and don't worry I am going to protect you from anyone who tries to take you away from me. Oh Hephaestion! I won't let you be alone so please don't let me be alone." Alexander had gone mad! What could I do to help him? He had too many enemies who would take advantage of him in this condition and if opportunity permitted they might well take his life.

Alexander scooted in next to me and lying on his side with his head resting on my shoulder he continued to talk to me. This went on for hours and when a friend would come respectfully (albeit somewhat fearfully) into the room to reason with him, he was sent packing with threats of death should he return. He would not allow food to be brought to the room saying he would eat when Hephaestion decided he was hungry.

"Remember Hephaestion how during our campaigns we relished a clear starlit night? We would walk off into the darkness away from the campfires until the only thing we heard was the sounds of the nocturnal. We would throw a cover on the ground and lie there together and see who could be first at spotting the little fireballs that race across the heavens.   Then because we had touched our legs together a little too much our flesh would stand up and lead us into a long bout of lovemaking. I remember the days when we were being schooled by Aristotle and you would charm him into letting us out early and we would go sailing. It was just the two of us and the ocean. There was the secret island, too small to be of any use but we knew what to use it for. You know I was just thinking that we should do that again if not on the ocean then maybe on the Euphrates. We were just past being children when we learned that we could pleasure each other and somehow we managed to do that several times a day. Remember when we visited the ruins of Troy and I laid a garland on Achilles' tomb and you on Patroclus, to show you were my beloved? Afterward we got naked in front of our soldiers and danced around the tomb. What a scandalous sensation that caused and we just laughed knowing that if all else was forgotten about us our naked dance would be remembered."

I didn't even think Alexander recalled those events but as the hours passed I relived my life with him through his words. He reflected on just the good times and the tender moments we had shared. He did not elaborate on his victories or titles given him. He talked as if the only thing that mattered in this whole world was what we had done together, nothing sad, no bitterness, but rather just how happy we had been. I found that since I had been pronounced dead, I loved him even more then I had before, if such a thing was possible.

For two days his madness persisted and he was inconsolable. He lay next to me swearing that he would not leave or eat until his father Zeus woke me up and we would dine together. He cried in my ear, begging me to awaken, and asking what he had done that I would not speak to him. He promised that if I would just be well again that he would declare me his co-regent. He pleaded with every Macedonian, Persian, and Indian god he could think of begging to give a year of his life for every year longer they would let me live. I wanted so much to speak to him and tell him that I was not really gone, only changed. My lips remained frozen and try as I might my voice stayed mute.

"Alexander, my great king, you knew Hephaestion better than any man and I venture to say even better than the god who made him." It was the soft deep voice of Aristenes. "Sire he would not want this for you or for him."

"Go away Aristenes. Leave us alone. We need to rest until he is better." Alexander said. He was not yelling or threatening the boy, for which I was grateful.

"Majesty there are things you must do and things you must know. While you were off on your campaign to make our world safer for us, I had the advantage of staying behind and studying at great expense to you and Hephaestion. In appreciation for you giving this humble servant such a gift I feel I must share with you some of what I learned." Here Aristenes paused and Alexander said nothing.

The youth continued, "In the library of Babylon is written all the knowledge accumulated over the ages in Persia and many other lands. One of the most sacred documents speaks of the treatment of a dead warrior. It says for a man to be elevated to the rank of hero his funeral plans must begin no later than three sunsets passed his death. I have conferred with scholars much more venerated than myself and they support this belief, not just in Persia but also in our motherland. Great Alexander, I truly fear that if you do not initiate funeral prayers and plans very quickly that Hephaestion will lose status with the gods. That will mean that you, as a divine deity, will not walk with Hephaestion when you join the gods. Of course my king you know what is best but I, upon fear for my life at interrupting your grief, had to tell this. With those words and your leave I will now depart from you sire. But may I first lay this garland at Hephaestion's feet and I have also brought one for you to place it at his head." I heard some movement. Alexander had given Aristenes permission to place the garland. Then I knew my young ward was walking away.

"Wait Aristenes, you are indeed a bold boy. I know why Hephaestion loved you. He taught me to love and trust you as well. If what you have told me is true and I've no doubt that you have been anything but honest with me we must get him declared a hero and arrangements must get under way!" Alexander had snapped out of his madness and I felt him running to the doors and yelling for attendants.

Aristenes had been amazing. I didn't know if what he had told Alexander was really archived in the library of Babylon or not. If it was not the boy had taken a great and deadly risk if he had been found out, but I had never in the years since I took him under my care (and body) caught him in so much as a mild exaggeration. He would truly have had a great future in our empire if we had lived.

My plans for a funeral did begin within the hour. If I had not realized my life was over before, I did now as they washed my body once again and anointed me with oils and dressed me in my most elaborate Chiliarch's uniform and cape. Golden necklaces were placed around my neck and Alexander's most valuable rings were placed on my fingers. Unlike most dead people I was able to hear the all the palace gossip as the servants worked around me. Most of the comments regarding me were positive. I was flattered by the comments they made about the size of my manhood as they washed it. They whispered about how full it must have made the Shahanshah feel and what an emptiness he must be experiencing. Others speculated that Aristenes would be my replacement. The thought of this did not bother me. Aristenes would be a good choice as long as Alexander did not take him against his will. I felt he would be especially adept at controlling some of the impetuousness of the king. There was fear, however, of Alexander and his moods without me as his consort. Imagine finally in death I was being referred to as Alexander's consort. In life it was not possible for me to be recognized as his husband, his equal perhaps but even Alexander could not get away with making me officially his mate. There was the whisper of wonder as to why my body was not corrupting; though Alexander was never asked about it, the popular opinion was that his divinity had put a halt to my body's decay. I would let them speculate on that. I was leaving my old life behind, I was lost to the man I had lived for, my wealth would be divided, I left a young wife of only four months still a virgin (I just never got around to it) and in mourning.

What would my future hold for me? I was wondering when I would have the mind contact with Xaphaxes and his two handsome friends. I had a thousand questions to which I needed answers. Foremost on my mind was when I would be able to go to Alexander and tell him I was alright and maybe we could be together again.

For my funeral arrangements Aristenes had become Alexander's secretary, of sorts. Any time the king was in my presence the boy was at his side writing down notes so that all of Alexander's wishes would be carried out. There were many wishes issued by the Shahanshah. As soon as preparations began Alexander had sent an envoy of messengers to the oracle of Siwa, to ask if Amon would permit me to be worshipped as a god. The reply came back that I might be worshipped as a divine hero, but not as a god. Alexander had expected this so he was happy. From that day forward my lover saw to it that I was honored with a hero's rites. He ordered that shrines were to be erected immediately to my memory throughout the world. Those orders took hold, as Hephaestion cults sprung up throughout the empire. Simple plaques are still being found in distant parts of the ancient world and some have made their way into modern museums. They are simply inscribed, "To the Hero Hephaestion".

Alexander ordered some things done of which I did not

approve. For example, the temple shrine of Asclepios and Ishtar in Ecbatana was ordered to be razed to the ground. That was a great loss; it was one of my last memories as a living person as I lay on my bed dying. Alexander was angered that the goddess, who could easily see into my room from her temple, did nothing to save me. He mandated laws of mourning to insure that everyone was aware of my loss. It was if to say if Alexander, Shahanshah of the world, cannot be happy then no one should be happy. The manes and tails of all horses were shorn, the battlements of neighboring cities were demolished, all ornamental carvings above doorways were chiseled away, and the banning of flutes or any kind of music was banned until Alexander decided to negate the order and the punishment for anyone being caught in the midst of laughter was arrest and public flogging. In a very sweet and sincere gesture Alexander had walked to my side once my body was completely prepared for display and taking a handful of his thick golden hair had cut it off with his dagger and placed it in my hand. I could feel the silkiness of the yellow locks and the roughness of his hands as he locked my stiff fingers around it. I actually still possess that lock of hair. What would that go for on eBay? I was to learn later that from that day forward Alexander was never without the necklace I had presented him in Egypt, made of gold strands and lapis with braids of my cock hair woven throughout.

Chapter Thirteen
On the Road to Babylon

There was growing amazement at the preservation of my body. I was in my sixth day of death and should have been quite aromatic by now. Normally there would have been great bronze vessels with smoky incense to camouflage the odor of decay, but in my case this was not necessary. An elaborate carriage had been constructed to carry my remains from Ecbatana to Babylon. Alexander himself drove the carriage taking turns with my beloved Aristenes. I could hear conversations between the two as the eight white horses decked in magnificent black plumes jostled us over the paved road. The two spoke as brothers without the formalities required in public places. Alexander did most of the talking, of course. He recounted our life together since we were twelve years old, leaving out few details. Aristenes listened with rapt attention taking in every word. Alexander was a gifted story teller and he was not shy about exaggerating some of our exploits. In truth he was making me sound better than I probably was. Memories have a tendency to be distorted either favorably or unfavorably depending on the individual's perception of the event. At any rate, if there were times that Alexander was not explicit enough about some episode Aristenes would interrupt him and ask him to elaborate on a point, to which the king was more than eager to do. When Alexander would start to sound too sad, Aristenes, gifted in the art of conversation, would ask Alexander questions that concerned only the king. I was surprised by the frankness of Alexander's openness. He told stories of his childhood that up until then only I had been privy. He spoke of his domineering mother and how she slept with a room full of snakes and often attempted sorcery without much success and how much nicer it was to hear her thoughts only through letters. He talked of Aristotle and what kind of man he was and how he had made both Alexander and me comfortable about physically loving each other passed the acceptable age. He did not dwell too much on his father, King Philip, only to say that he and I had accomplished in five years what his father had failed to do in his entire lifetime.

But Alexander would not stay on the subject of himself long before weaving his story so as to include me. By the end of the second day he was sharing intimate details with Aristenes. If I had not been dead I know I would have blushed. He told him about the secret rooms we had found as boys in the royal palace. They could be accessed in council chambers by moving a discretely placed stone and the whole wall would pivot with a light touch. We had discovered them quite by accident when playing around. It was obvious by the dust covering ancient furniture that these rooms had not been visited probably for generations. He told Aristenes that in there was where we would sneak when we wanted to pleasure each other, often two or three times a day. It was in these rooms that the young prince had first approached me about putting his cock in my backside. Alexander had Aristenes' full attention on that story. He told the youth about how I had allowed him to put his fingers in me but he could not imagine something as large as his cock going in there. No matter how much he promised it would not hurt and that he had seen soldiers do it to each other and they seemed to like it, I would not budge. One day when we two had been out riding and returned to the stables Alexander had made the opportunity to prove his point. There was a young slave whose job was just to see to his horse, Bucephalus, needs. This young slave was probably passed his twentieth year as he sported the shadow of a full beard. Alexander explained to Aristenes that the two of us took the slave to a room in the back of the stables where sundry horse paraphernalia was kept and ordered him to strip. As a slave the young man had no choice but to do so without question. Stripped, it was easy to tell the prince had chosen well; the stable boy was lean with muscles lying tightly below the skin. His complexion was olive, as were most of the slaves captured from time to time in the Roman peninsula, his chest smooth and his back broad without the marks of a whip that were usually found on male slaves. His legs were slender but shapely in their musculature and covered with curly black hair making them very manly. Like most of the men from his area of the world his cock was thick and long with low hanging balls and surrounded in a thick patch of jet black hair.

"Hephaestion was rather naïve in those days and asked me what I meant to do." Alexander confided to my ward. As soon I as could come back to life I was going to talk to him about this. "I explained to him that we were going to learn how to fuck a man. It was unthinkable that we could spend our life together and Hephaestion not expect me to bury my cock in him from time to time. Of course he protested and said if I was going to put mine in him then he should be allowed to do the same to me. Of course, I reminded him that someday I was going to be his king and could do it to him anyway but then I paused and added…we'll see. This seemed to satisfy him. I told Hephaestion, that we should probably have him suck us first and ordered him on his knees in front of us. I am yet indebted to this slave so I should use his name." Alexander said. "He came from a noble family and I quite honestly don't know his full name, but we called him Pax, which in his language is supposed to mean peace. I had always liked him and favored him by making the care of Bucephalus his only duty. Actually he rides with us now as a loyal soldier. Anyway, I had dropped my breechcloth and indicated to Hephaestion to do the same. I ordered Pax to start with me. He walked over to me on his knees and took my flaccid pole into his mouth working his tongue to the base and back to the tip. As it began to rise he took his hand to hold it steady so that he could work his tongue into my foreskin and use his lips to push it back from the crown. My sensitive head uncovered and his broad tongue laving it had me at my full size. I told him to do the same to Hephaestion and as he did I took Hephaestion's hand and brought it to my cock so he could stroke me while I watched Pax pleasure him. My handsome slave was the only man other than me to pleasure Hephaestion up to that time. Pax was making my man feel very good. I could tell by the way Hephaestion's knees were bent and he was thrusting with such vigor into Pax's mouth that the poor youth had to grasp the back of Hephaestion's still boyishly smooth thighs to maintain his balance."

Alexander stopped telling the story at this point because an officer rode up to the side of my funeral carriage and quietly asked Alexander when we could make camp for the night. Alexander advised him that we should travel for two more hours and for him to send some men ahead to set up camp and as the night before I was to be placed in Alexander's tent so that he could personally guard my body. By travelling two more hours Alexander felt that if we started early enough the following day we should enter the gates of

Babylon at high noon. He also told the officer that after some rest tonight that he should send a squadron of men ahead to Babylon to ensure that the entire population would be lining the boulevard to the palace to show me proper respect. With those orders the soldier rode off to see them carried through. Alexander and Aristenes continued with me on the bumpy road in silence.

"Please my king, finish your story about Pax. I fear that if you don't tell me now I will never know what happened." Aristenes asked respectfully. I knew what was happening. While grieved, both men were sitting in the carriage seat horny and hard from what Alexander had been saying and me lying dead in a golden box behind them. In truth, that memory had me horny to, but my poor retched cock just lay next to my thigh without so much as a twitch.

Alexander chuckled quietly at the boy's request but continued where he had left off. "Well, not wanting your sponsor to lose his seed quite yet, I simply told Pax to stop and commanded him to bend over a post, which was secured to two wooden supports used for slinging horse leathers on for cleaning. Pax did as I told him with his feet wide apart. He had a beautiful muscular ass that was smooth and cushioned out, which was perfect padding for any pelvis that might be slamming into it. I should tell you that it had been in the back of my mind for some time to use Pax in order to get my point across about the benefits of being fucked. I knew Pax would not show pain when we shoved our inexperienced staffs into him. I knew this, not because I had fucked him before, but because not many weeks before that day, I had gone to the stables to get Bucephalus when I heard sounds coming from the very room Hephaestion and I were now. I walked quietly to the door and unnoticed peeped around the corner. To my surprise there was my father and a young general out of tunics. My father was thrusting his cock in and out of Pax with all his force while his general, Craterus (one of my own generals now) stood in front of the lad. With every thrust forward King Philip was pushing Pax's open mouth over the prick of Craterus. I watched this for about twenty minutes before Philip slowed down and his trusts became more thoughtful. He was pulling his manhood out to where just the tip was touching the youth's asshole followed by a complete re-entry past the muscle ring and to his cock's base. He did this type of penetration repeatedly until he began to moan in earnest and with one final push he held on to the boy's waist and held himself there. I could tell my father was shooting spurt after spurt into the young man's ass. All through this Pax had been moaning and begging for more. When my father pulled out I noticed that he had been blessed by the same gods as me. I wasn't quite as big as him yet but I knew I would be. My father put his uniform back on and told the general to do as he would with Pax with the caveat that under no circumstance was he to hurt him as he was my slave. Philip told his general that he was leaving since he had no desire to watch his perversions. Then he laughed and started to walk toward the door I had been hiding by.

Well, I actually did want to stay and watch Craterus and find out about this perversion of which my father spoke. So getting behind a leather smith's table and remaining in the shadows my father walked right passed me. As soon as I was certain he was gone I went back to my place by the door, where there was a gap large enough for me to see through without being easily found out. When I looked back in the room Pax was standing and facing the man. Craterus was a giant of a man with huge muscles and truly had the gruff commanding voice of a general. His men respected him but they feared him as well, having seen him in battle with only his hands to fight with. It is said that he killed three men with his bare hands before his soldiers could get to him. I was glad my father had given him orders not to hurt Pax, because I knew he would follow those instructions. "

"But what did he want to do?" an excited Aristenes asked.

"Patience Aristenes, I will get to that." Alexander cautioned. It was strange for me to hear the word patience coming from my beloved. "I must advise you Aristenes, I am about to reward you with a story that is only known by Pax, myself and Hephaestion…" Alexander caught himself. "That is just Pax, Craterus, and I know this story so you must never divulge anything that I tell you, but especially this since Craterus still lives and is a valuable officer" Aristenes assured him that nothing the three of us had said or done and certainly not stories from Hephaestion's boyhood would ever escape his lips. I knew Alexander smiled at him and squeezed his thigh. He knew a secret was safe with Aristenes or I would never have brought the boy into his life.

"Craterus was talking to Pax in that deep baritone voice, much like you will have some day I think. He told Pax he knew what to do and that he did not have much time as there was a celebration scheduled to take place at the general's house that night celebrating the birth of his seventh son.

"I understand my general. Are you ready?" Pax asked him.

"Yes." Craterus said. His voice sounded higher and quieter.

"What are you doing out of your uniform you fat pig?" Yelled my slave Pax at the highest ranking general in Macedonia, in a voice I had never heard from Pax.

Craterous was cowering even as he answered. "I forgot that you were coming sir and I was going to go with the men to clean ourselves."

"You lie to me Craterus. When will you ever learn to be truthful with me? You are such a disgrace." Pax screamed at him and I nearly yelled out when the handsome slave boy walked over to the general and slapped him hard across his cheek. Craterous winced and began to sob, holding his hand against his reddening face.

"You are right father. I have once again been disobedient. I don't want to be a disgrace to you or to my uniform. Help me be good. Please father." Craterus begged dropping to his knees. I thought my ears deceiving me. My father's general calling this man who two years ago just turned to a man 'father'. Craterus could easily have been his father.

"We have obviously been remiss in teaching you how to be a man. Unfortunately you are the one who must be disciplined and not me. Stand up and bend over that post." Pax ordered. Once the general had followed the command Pax gathered some leather straps, easily found in a stable, and tied the large man to the post. Pax, I knew, had done this before. He was much too calm to be tying up a man, who normally had the authority to have him executed without a king's trial. After checking to see that the man was securely bound, Pax walked to a wooden trunk and pulled out a whip, which he carried smugly around to the front of the general, smacking it against the palm of his hand one whack at a time.

"This is what I would like to use on you for being such a disobedient son! I would like to lash your back until it bleeds and laugh while I rub pepper oil into the wounds. You wouldn't want your little soldier friends to see that his father had whipped the big man until he bled would you?"

"No father," Craterus whimpered.

"If I did that to you then they would all know how bad a person your father thinks you are, wouldn't they son?" Oozed out the words from my horse's servant.

"Yes father they would know and they must never know. Please, please don't do that father!"

"I won't. Not because I care about hurting you but because it would disgrace me more if those soldiers found out what a woman you really were. It would get so bad for you that every time they had you in the right place they would use you like a whore. It would be so bad for you that you would have to run your sword through your own gut." Pax was good. "Do you want that Craterus? I have other sons and they are men. The stigma would eventually leave my family after I publicly disowned you."

"No! No! Please do anything you want." Craterus said in a shrill voice. This must have been the answer Pax was awaiting, because he smiled, walked over to the box, lay the whip down, and picked up a narrow board wrapped in leather.

"This is going to sting your ass until you will wish you were dead, but it will leave not marks." Pax explained as he bent over and picked the thong up that he had worn all day while working the stables, wadded it up and forced it into the general's mouth. Now the officer not being able to scream for help just waited. The wait did not last long. From behind him Pax swung the leather paddle. When it contacted the muscular ass of the man he tried to cry out but the gag held the sound in his throat. Again the paddle came down and suddenly Pax was not waiting the customary time between swats for he started doing one after the other in quick succession until I counted thirty. The general was hanging somewhat limp but was no longer crying. True to Pax's promise the skin was not broken but there were great red welts that would be gone by morning but would stay sore for a while.

Pax then walked over to him and shook him, he was still quite groggy. "Craterus I need you at attention I have more I need to tell you. I know what will wake you." My slave walked to within two feet of the general's back and still being unclothed, Pax took his thick long cock in his hand and began to piss on the general's back. He waved his pole up and down and side to side covering Craterus' entire backside with the golden liquid. There must have been a few spots with broken skin because when the yellow piss touched certain areas Craterus revived and Pax pulled the ball of sweat covered rag from his mouth.

"There now son, do you think you have learned your lesson?

"I do. I do think I have learned it this time father. Untie me please and I will go back to my troops.

"I think one more lesson needs to be done before I free you." Pax stated almost agreeably.

Agitation and fear appeared on Craterus' face. "No more father. Please."

Pax paid him no mind and dipping his hand into a vat of leather oil, he liberally applied some to his fleshpole, which was raging and enormous, and he ladled more of the oil down the arsecrack of the writhing begging general. Without ceremony, Pax rammed what I am sure was over nine inches of Roman cocked up the general's ass. The youth let his member lay in the general for several seconds before imitating exactly the way my father had fucked him just a short while ago. In fact I thought I could see the glistening of my father's fluid as it ran out of Pax's hole and down his leg. The rhythm was barely started when Craterus began to moan in ecstasy and pushing his ass back toward his assaulter to get every last bit of the boy into him. Pax was getting out of breath he was fucking so hard but still in character said. "I'm going to shoot some of my seed up your ass in hopes you will absorb it and become a smarter more obedient son." With those words Pax stuck his staff in as far as it would go and shot his essence into the moaning general. Pax pulled out undid the ties and ordered the general to clean him and himself up and get back to his soldiers and that he didn't want to see him again.

Craterus got some clean rags and wet them, on his knees he worked at cleaning the oil sperm mixture off the boy's cock. Then he turned him around and pulled the young ass cheeks apart and appeared to be cleaning my father's essence from the boy with his tongue. When Pax walked away and picked up his clothing and began getting dressed Craterus looked over to him with downcast eyes.

"Pax I would like to ask you one more thing." Craterus said to the boy.

"Yes my general. Whatever you want to ask of me you have

but to do." Pax answered as a subservient once more.

"I want to swallow your essence before I leave. I don't know how long I will be gone with Philip this time." Craterus stated flatly in his deep general's voice one again.

"I would be honored General." Pax the slave told Craterus the general.

Pax's cock had not really gone down since fucking the older man. I was wondering if he had actually spurted in the general's ass or just made it look so. In an instant Craterus was on his knees before the handsome young man and without wasting any time had swallowed the boy's staff to the root. The general was an expert. I could tell by the expressions on the slave's face that it was really giving him pleasure. His knees had gotten kind of wobbly but he wasn't thrusting himself into the general's throat as most men do. He really did not have to with Craterus' head doing it for him. I noted that Craterus had moved his pointing finger behind the boy and had slipped it into Pax's ass and this really had my stable boy moaning. It was not long before Pax could not contain himself and began shooting a load into the general's mouth. The soldier worked hard to swallow it all but still some seeped from around his lips and slowly ran down into his beard. He stood up without words and finished dressing while Pax did the same. Then Craterus walked over to the boy placed his hands on his shoulders and stunned me with his words.

"Pax you know I love you."

"And I love you Craterus." Craterus pulled him forward to give the boy a kiss but before he could Pax reached up and with two of his fingers wiped the essence from his black beard and stuck them in the general's mouth where he quickly leaked them clean. Now they kissed long and deeply. Then Craterus turned his back and walked out, while I remained out of sight."

Alexander stopped the wagon for a few minutes and ordered some wine brought to both of them. After they had jumped down from the carriage seat and walked a respectable distance from my remains they each emptied their bladder and, knowing my boys, they were standing there pissing through swollen cocks resulting from Alexander's storytelling and taking quick note of each other's equipment just to confirm it hadn't changed since that time in Egypt.

Back on the road we had only about an hour to travel before reaching camp. "Please Alexander I want to hear the finish of the meeting of the two of you with Pax." Aristenes insisted. So there was still a bit of the inquisitive youth that I had saved from an inconsequential life of drudgery where his great mind would never have been used. He was growing into a man whom Alexander and I could both be proud to have adopted into our family.

"There isn't much more to tell Aristenes. But rather than having you speculate on what happened, I will finish the story. So Pax had leaned over the rail offering us his cute little ass. I decided I should be the first to go since Hephaestion would know if he could take my cock without complaint there must not be too much involved with being fucked. I did what I had seen Pax do some time back and oiled my pole with leather oil and of course I showed Hephaestion how to apply oil to the young slave's hole. I did this as if I was quite experienced but in fact I was just imitating what I had witnessed. Remember you always must have a goal and mine was to fuck Hephaestion's ass, even if

I had to beg him on my knees publicly in my father's throne room. With Hephaestion standing to my side watching I guided my cock to the tight little hole between Pax's ass cheeks. I had peeled the foreskin back on my stallion and placed the tip at the boy's entrance. As I pushed in we could hear a slight gasp from Pax. As you may recall Aristenes my cockhead is large and somewhat blunt, so it takes quite a bit of pressure to pass it through the muscle ring. Once I had passed that strategic point Pax sighed and began pushing back against me to the point he was crushing the curls of hair at the base of my cock. I then began to fuck in earnest. It was my first time and I felt like my father Zeus was hitting me with lightning volts of ecstasy. I was very young and was so excited that the thrill did not last long, because I shot my seed in the man quicker than I like to say. When I had finished I still had that exquisite afterglow and I leaned over and lay on Pax's back until it had passed. I pulled out with a wet noise. I told Pax to stay in place because my friend was going to practice fucking on him.

Hephaestion offered no resistance at being initiated in the fine art of man on man fucking. He didn't last much longer than I had but we had a good boyish time. I got a rag and wiped Hephaestion off and he did the same for me. Pax had stood up and turned around with a big smile on his face. He was bending over to retrieve his clothing when Hephaestion and I both noticed his enormous erection. This young man was not only large soft but when he was hard he was easily nine or ten inches and his cock sprung out from the most glorious thatch of glossy black hair. I asked Hephaestion if he would like to share some essence with me. We were both on our knees so fast in front of Pax that I think we scared him. We both started licking his shaft, we would get to its base and then licking on each side we would work our way up to the tip and try to kiss each other with the tip between our lips. After a while we began licking up the olive skinned smoothness that was his chest to the small brown button teats that we bit and nibbled on mercilessly. Finally, we made it to his armpits, which were covered in silky black hair. He smelled of fresh man sweat and we licked him clean with relish. We then had him lie on this back Hephaestion laid between his legs, which as I described earlier were unbelievably hairy. Hephaestion was going wild from the tickling sensations Pax's wiry leg hair was creating against his tender sides and young hairless thighs. I was working on his pole. He started writhing and when Hephaestion felt his balls, which he was sucking, retreat up he scooted up and we shared the head of that fat Roman cock until ropes of his thick white seed was feeding us. We both lapped it up like it was the last honey on earth. What essence we had not swallowed was on our face. I asked Pax to lick it off and he seemed to enjoy doing it. We dressed and went about our day. That was not the last time we used Pax as a source of sexual knowledge. When I became king I decided to let Pax earn his freedom through military service. I assigned him to Craterus as a soldier and personal assistant.

So Aristenes, what do you think of our little learning experiment with a stable boy?"

"He was one very lucky boy to have been chosen by the two of you to learn on. Did it help Hephaestion get over his fear? Asked Aristenes.

Alexander laughed. "From that day on we were like hares in the field. Hephaestion never said no again."

Alexander had assembled thirty thousand of his finest soldiers to escort us to the gates of Babylon. Many were our

Companions, who out of respect dedicated themselves and their arms to me. Alexander had made it known that there would never be a replacement appointed to take my place as commander of the Companion cavalry, but that my name was to be preserved always in connection with it and so Hephaestion's Regiment it continued to be called and my image was to continue to be carried before it. All of my escort were dressed in their finest and as ordered travelled the three day journey in complete silence with only the clomping of hooves and the occasional snort from a disrespectful horse could be heard.

Chapter Fourteen
The Gates of Babylon

Just as Alexander planned, my funeral carriage arrived at high noon. The sound of horns heralded my entry into the city followed by the moans of sorrow from tens of thousands of citizens and slaves alike. Alexander's messengers had prepared the population well. While I could not see what was going on I was able to imagine and my assumptions were later confirmed to me. People were everywhere, on roof tops, along the wide boulevard leading to the royal palace, windows, balconies, and doorways. To the right stood the magnificent and celebrated Hanging Gardens of Babylon, one of the wonders of the ancient world. Babylonians worshipped many gods and as a result there were many temples, all of which were smoking from incense that would carry the priest's prayers to the heavens. Alexander was in full military dress and I could only imagine how beautiful he must have looked. He had insisted on driving the carriage by himself. Aristenes wore the clothing of an aristocrat and walked behind my funeral carriage carrying a torch. In turn he was followed by soldiers on horseback, who rode in pairs. These dual sets of soldiers numbered fifteen thousand long, making this a sea of humanity for as far as the eye could see.

Alexander had Aristenes brought to his tent early that morning and told him the entry plan. He had told him that he would like to have him on the carriage next to him but that the citizens would think him just a servant. He felt that being torch bearer, which was a position of great honor, would gain him recognition. He further told him that unlike what had been discussed in the past, he would not be serving in our army. I could feel the beautiful young man's disappointment and the start of a verbal protest, which he muted under the circumstances. He wanted very much to be one of Alexander's warriors. I had of course always made certain that he was never in harm's way. As I mentioned earlier, he was the one physically perfect and pure hearted possession in my life. Alexander went on after a pause for he could well empathize with the young man's desire to prove himself a warrior.

"Aristenes, I know what the call of battle feels like. You have always made it clear that you wanted to be in my army. I cannot think of another man, beside Hephaestion, who would be a more loyal comrade in battle than you. But I must follow up with what Hephaestion would want me to do for he shared with me all of his heart's desires. He wanted you to travel to distant lands and represent us. He felt that some battles could be won more solidly through diplomacy rather than war and he had proven himself right on this point many times. You will be given the title prince and it will eventually be announced that you are Hephaestion's heir as his adopted son. Believe me when I tell you, Aristenes, that you will be more powerful than any warrior. For your words and reports to me will determine the fates of nations; they will carry enough weight to help me decide if I can welcome a conquest into my empire peacefully or if we release my army upon them like a plague. You have never been a slave to us, but I want you to know that you are free to do what you like with your life. You have the education and the mind to be a scholar and a teacher, perhaps as great as Aristotle, you can go home to Macedonia where you will be wealthy and revered, you are free to marry a woman and have children for whom you can build a great estate, or you can join my family as a great diplomat as Hephaestion envisioned. What say you?"

"I don't know what to say." The forever truthful Aristenes replied. "I never let myself think that I could possibly accomplish more than to ride with you and my beloved Hephaestion into battle. I realize now that will never happen.

I have no desire to go home and simply be a rich man. As far as marriage and children, my taste for sexual pleasure has never included a woman. The thought of being Hephaestion's brother is more of an honor than I can possibly be worthy of being given. I choose to be your family and to be of whatever service I can be."

"Then it is done Aristenes or should I say Prince Aristenes of the House of Hephaestion?" Asked Alexander, who I could hear patting the boys back. "You will need to wear these clothes that I had brought from my wardrobe."

"Yes my king. May I ask you one more thing?" I was hoping Aristenes wasn't going to push it. I knew that Alexander was very stressed and had sobbed most of the night, as he lay next to my coffin.

"Yes." Alexander said followed by "But be quick, we have much to do this day."

"Promise me that you will never make me marry a woman." Aristenes just threw this one out. I doubt anyone beside me or Alexander's mother had ever asked the Shahanshah to promise anything just to be doing it.

This actually got a laugh out of Alexander. "Aristenes perhaps you are more than just adopted by Hephaestion. No, I will never force a woman on you. You are much too nice and they would devour you like an Egyptian crocodile after a Nile swimmer. After a respectable time you can take a man as your own or live without the constraints of a relationship. I told you that you are free."

"I don't think I ever want another man. I prefer to live with the memory of Hephaestion and those memories will be enough." Aristenes said he voice heavy with sorrow.

"I know how you feel Aristenes. My world is without meaning now. I don't know what my destiny holds from here." Alexander's voice was trembling and I could feel the weight of his loneliness. Aristenes was quick to pick up on the changing mood.

"Majesty allow me to help you get in those vestments. You've no idea the impact you have on your subjects when you dress in this fashion." Aristenes said picking up the leather tunic with its bronze studs.

Slightly relaxed Alexander accepted the help. "Aristenes, you must promise me one thing. That you will practice on not being so nice. We will talk about it later. Let's get going you know how much Hephaestion liked punctuality."

We arrived at the palace, where my enclosed remains were gently removed, placed on a litter with long poles, and hoisted on the shoulders of twenty young men and carried to the center of the great throne room where I was to lie in state until my funeral pyre was made ready and the fire would turn my flesh to ash. Alexander had me placed in such a position that he would be able to sit on his throne and see me as well as the face of every man who walked by to pay last respects. He also wasted no time issuing orders creating memorials throughout his empire in my name. All artists who were masters at the art of sculpturing were conscripted at whatever cost to make my likeness which would be distributed to the ends of the world. My love employed Stasicrates, an artist famous for his innovations, which combined an exceptional degree of magnificence, audacity and ostentation to design a funeral pyre unlike the world had ever seen.

The pyre was 180 feet high, square in shape, and built in stepped levels. The first level was decorated with two hundred and forty ships with golden prows, each of these adorned with armed figures, and with red banners filling the spaces between. On the second level were torches, with snakes at the base, golden wreaths in the middle, and at the top, flames surmounted by eagles. The third level showed a hunting scene and the fourth a battle of centaurs, all done in gold. On the fifth level, also in gold, were lions and bulls, and on the sixth, the arms of Macedon and Persia. The seventh and final level bore sculptures of sirens, hollowed out to conceal a choir who would sing a lament. When the choir was finished after several hours of singing their farewell to a hero, they would exit and Alexander would use a torch, whose fire was to be brought from the temple of Apollo, and light my pyre.

Before the days of the actual cremation Alexander ordered funeral games to be held in my honor. The contests ranged from literature to athletics, and three thousand competitors took part, the festival eclipsed anything that had gone before, both in cost and in numbers taking part. Today's historians estimate that the cost of my funeral would be almost three billion dollars.

When the day of the cremation came, Alexander ordered everyone from the pyre and he walked alone, requesting that even Aristenes not accompany him, to the top where my body lay in the open on an ornately carved wooden platform. My body (well dressed that it was) covered simply by my cloak, which Alexander gently raised and lowered it below my waist. I still clasped his locks of golden hair in my hands that were in exactly the position Alexander himself had placed them. He had decided that my burning would be at night so that the gods and everybody else would not miss the glow of the flames. It was a clear night and the stars shone brightly there was no moon. I could feel him stare down at me for a long period of time. He was leaned over me in the silence that was his new companion these last weeks. Not a word did he speak, but I could feel the drops of tears falling on my face. Inside I was crying with him and I had the strongest sense that I was deceiving him. At long last I felt him kiss me, as he stood up, I heard him sniff in a fashion that meant he was pulling himself together so that he could face his men who waited at the base of the pyre.

"Hephaestion you were everything to me and I promise you the world will never forget you. I promise you that somehow, even if I have to defy the gods, I will be with you again someday. I will take care of your little Aristenes though he is as big as you. Farewell for a short while." With those words Alexander turned and walked to the stairs.

One final tribute remained that eventually would have the whole empire talking about the high esteem in which Alexander held me. When he exited the base of the pyre, horns began to sound. It was the signal to follow his orders that the sacred flame in every temple should be extinguished. This was traditionally only to be done on the death of the great king himself.

The flaming torch was handed to Alexander who clasped it in his strong hands and walking to an opening at the base of the pyre he touched the fire to the kindling beneath the structure and the fire began to spread throughout the first level. Each level had been strategically oiled to feed the flames. Soon, it was as if a million golden tongues were lapping at the structure. True to its design, as the hours went on, each smaller level fell into the level below it. My crematorium had been built on a small plateau a mile from the gates to Babylon. Alexander had been prudent enough not to construct the edifice where the city would be in danger of going up in ashes with me. All the time it was burning the wails of sorrow from the thousands of people could be heard.

On a distant bluff, my three friends and I watched as I was transformed from flesh to a memory. Before dawn broke over the horizon we were gone, not from fear of light but that we may not be seen.

Chapter Fifteen
The Awakening

The acropolis on which my pyre had been build was also the sight of a former temple, whose existence had been forgotten many ages ago. There was no way the untrained eye could detect that the rocks scattered there had at one time been a part of a vast complex. Of course, Xaphaxes had been there on several occasions. He said it felt like yesterday, but was in fact over four thousand years ago. It had been our good fortune that my pyre had been built there because there still existed underground passageways that my friends had easily reopened to facilitate an unnoticed exit from the flames.

No sooner had Alexander made his departure than my three friends stood by my side. Xaphaxes wasted no time in bending over and inserting his fangs into my neck injecting the serum that would take my paralysis away. I was told that during my paralysis my body had totally transformed. The fact that I had been fed the blood of Xaphaxes and two of the oldest vampires on earth would work in my favor to make me all but invincible. I revived quickly and following my creators down the stairs to the first level was taken to a great golden statue of the goddess Isis which they were easily able to push aside and just as the flames began to appear down a shaft we jumped. Xaphaxes led us through a maze of underground corridors that had not been walked in for thousands of years, until we came to a small opening that led to the outside at the base of the plateau. From there at lightning speed we went for some distance and from there we watched. The world that Alexander and I had created was already beginning to end.

As I watched the fire and listened to the sorrowful moans of the populace, I of course knew that they had been told to cry. It was our way. But I wondered of those men standing with Alexander, who stood there so handsomely all the while his wet silent tears glistening in the firelight, truly mourned with him. Then I was able to hear them think. Most of my men were feeling sadness. Some wondered what would become of them without me for just as today, life then was just as uncertain. I had earned the respect if not the love of most of our soldiers and even the diplomats at court, but you can't please everyone and I could hear my detractor's thoughts as well. Some men that Alexander and I had really trusted had already begun thinking of ways to bring the great Alexander down and grab what was his and take for themselves. Craterus, whom I had gifted with Pax, was afraid that with me out of the picture Alexander would be out of control and destroy himself. The old general decided there at my funeral fire that he would retire from the army and with Pax go to some distant corner of the empire where his wife and kids would not know about and where Pax could treat him like the bad boy he was. The only thing the artist Stasicrates was crying about was that his greatest work of art, gaudy as it may have been was so short lived as the flames brought it to the ground. Perdiccas, a friend and confidante of mine, truly was mourning me. Above all the genuine cries to reach my mind were the sad prayers of Aristenes, who stood dazed next to Alexander. My poor man-boy was sending prayers to gods who could not hear them because they didn't exist. This was when the realization that he would never see me again, truly became real to him. As caught up as Alexander was in his feeling of desolation, I think he felt the boy's thoughts and knew that this young man loved me as much as he had loved me and yet Alexander did not perceive it as a threat, which indeed it wasn't. My dear sweet Alexander, in one of those rare moments when he was not caught up into himself, discreetly reached over in the darkness and intertwined his fingers with those of Aristenes.

Our trip was swift, as the three ancient Quermen took me to the Habitat. There my instructions began. Just as Xaphaxes had done four thousand years earlier, I went through a similar regiment. My three inseparable men taught me how to hunt and to choose my victims wisely. If I must kill to feed I was to be fast and merciful, under most circumstances. I was from day one to make an effort not to kill, to control my thirst and leave things as I found them as much as possible. The Quermen cautioned that they believed everyone we killed changed the future and the world might lose a valuable person. At the same time they said killing might be doing the world a favor. They told me eventually I would need only drops to live but that it would be a while.

I had been at the Habitat for probably three months, absorbing everything these ancient beings felt they should impart to me. I was advised that some things would probably not be shared with me for decades perhaps centuries, as the Tribunal of Twelve took into consideration my works. Since sleep was not something I needed to do any longer, I had twenty four hours a day to learn. Just as in humans, there is a difference in learning capacity and ability. My mentors were complimentary about my propensity for fact absorption and how easily I could profile situations. This they said was critical for my survival. Languages were simple; if you can read the mind you can produce the appropriate sounds. I was taught philosophies and science from civilizations so old that the world no longer has record of them. Even Atlantis, yes it did exist, was young when compared to the origins of some of my teachers at the habitat. I went after everything I could glean from the Quermen. Some of their advice and caveats I put to the back of my mind. I was, after all, still a spoiled boy at heart. This would cause me some difficulties over the centuries. It has not been a few times that I have been called before the Tribunal of Twelve for some indiscretions that I may have committed in my zest to be a pioneer. I am sure that if they had known that a mere twenty three hundred years in the future I would be writing this story with plans of more books about our world to come, the consequences would have been dire.

By the end of the third month my constant training was ending and I was going to be able to specialize in matters of interest to me. With Xaphaxes, Anak, and Maneti, I was brought before the Tribunal of Twelve (It is called a tribunal because the twelve consisted of three sets of four. Each set of four represented a different politic. I suppose the best way of putting it is that one set was liberal, one moderate, and one conservative. Each set would consider a circumstance and would debate its merit and application to Quermen belief. In the end two of the three sets could lean in any direction making the outcome completely unpredictable but fair) The Tribunal of Twelve wanted to simply ask if my inclination was to remain in the Habitat or if I felt directed to live in the outside among humankind. I immediately responded that I must live on the outside and that I had traveled the world since I was a youth and had no desire to stay in one place, at least for the foreseeable future. I also told them I had unfinished obligations and that I must see to those.

"Hephaestion, we would not try to persuade you to stay at the Habitat against your will. You have a brilliant mind, one of the most outstanding prodigies to enter our society in millennia, and we hope that one day when the time is right for you that you will join us here. The work that can be done from here contributes as much as any Quermen on the outside." The Tribunal of Twelve spoke to my mind as one. "If you follow our guidelines, there is nothing in the world out there that cannot be yours for the asking and at the same time you can be of benefit both to our race and human kind. It is our belief that the world would evolve differently than it is going to if more Quermen walked the earth, but most of the exceptionally gifted choose a cloistered existence. Out there you will find Quermen who have turned toward a deviant way of life. While we are not human some of us let our power corrupt. You must be very careful of these Quermen, whom we have named Religrites. They will try to convert you to their beliefs and if you don't see life their way they will try make their followers hate you and even take your life. You must let us know where you have located one and we will take him from the world and stop the spread of his poison.

In regards to your unfinished affairs, all of those were finished for you the moment you died. If you leave here, you must go far away from everything you knew so that you won't be tempted to contact those who knew you in life. You must not return to places where you were known until it is certain that those humans have grown old and died. In your earthly situation you were known throughout the world. It would therefore be prudent that you stay here at Habitat until no less than fifty years have passed, when you may safely leave here and live among humans without fear of recognition."

As you can imagine the thoughts of being only here for another half century, as peaceful and tranquil as it was, did not sit well with me. "In all due respect Tribunal of Twelve, I would surely go into madness if I were to be expected to stay here without physically being in the world I left. I must see Alexander and let him know I am with him. I can hear his grieving when I listen. My hope is to make him Quermen."

I think I had elicited the first audible gasp the Tribunal of Twelve had made in twenty thousand years. My mentors standing at my side were just as shocked. "Hephaestion that is the very last thing you should consider doing. We cannot allow that. The subject is dropped." With those words to me, the Tribunal of Twelve stood and was gone. I was swept from the chamber of the Tribunal of Twelve by my mentors and taken back to my own suite of rooms.

"What did I say?"

"Hephaestion, I really wish that you had consulted with us before suggesting that you were going to give the gift to Alexander." Xaphaxes said.

"If we had just known that you were considering that we could have warned you against such a rash action." The beautiful Maneti said to me in a somewhat patronizing tone.

"I don't understand." I said, the surprise still in my voice. "It is certainly no secret that I love Alexander. I have not given my heart to any other since I was a child. I would think that with all the knowledge sequestered in the Habitat that it would have dawned on one of the minds in here that now that I am going to live forever I would want Alexander at my side. I cannot even begin to contemplate an eternity without him. Explain to me why this is not possible!" I demanded.

"Well, in the first place a novice is not normally permitted to give the gift to a human for several generations. In the second place anyone being given the gift normally must meet certain criteria, and finally the Tribunal of Twelve must give consent." Explained Xaphaxes. He of course knew that I had been taught that. But as with everything I had shrugged it off knowing that circumstances always allowed for exceptions to the rule. I thought this would certainly be true for the second most powerful man in the world…that is until I had died. But I still felt that I should carry some clout.

I asked. "But I am capable of giving the gift. Am I not?"

"You know you are. It is just not wise. You are very powerful because the three of us gave you our blood, but you in turn will not have blood that powerful to share for a long time. Anyone you turn will not have your strength for at least a thousand years and that makes them more susceptible to the persuasion of the Religrites." Replied Maneti.

"I cannot accept that. If that is true, you can come with me and give him the gift just as you gave it to me." I told them.

"That will not be possible. It took all the power of persuasion and logic that the three of us possessed to present you to the Tribunal of Twelve as a candidate for the gift. It was with some reservation, due to your impending death, that the Tribunal of Twelve leaned our way and allowed us to make you Quermen. Until today's meeting they have been completely impressed with you." Maneti advised me.

"You three have each other. Why must I be denied the comfort of having Alexander?" I yelled.

"Because, Hephaestion, Alexander is a monster!" Shouted Anak, who had been quiet until now. "Have you learned nothing from us here? We are a society who has risen from violence. We destroyed our civilization with violence. We have spent untold ages bringing our baser desires under control. You personally are experiencing, even now, the lust for blood. The need to quench that thirst is a constant reminder to us of the violent past we share. The need to feed off the living should be repugnant to you. You must always keep in mind even as you feed on a buck in the forest that its blood is not truly yours to take. So that when you suggest bringing a creature like Alexander into our midst we are appalled."

I was angered and confused at Anak's words. "How can you judge Alexander that way? He is bringing peace to the world. He is uniting countries that were once enemies. He seeks to make all men brothers."

"Hephaestion use that great mind of yours. You hear from Alexander only what you choose, which is the loss he feels for you. Don't you realize that mankind may not want to be the brothers that Alexander envisions for them? Just as the Religrites, who want to control all that their followers think or do, that is what Alexander is doing to the world. His power had made him a madman, his policies are as changeable as the weather, and his anger in the form of justice is swift and murderous. Not long after your funeral fire, did you know that he led an assault on a tribe called the Cossaeans, who offered surrender and no resistance, and he had every man, woman, and child massacred as an offer to the spirit of you, Hephaestion? In his insanity he thought that he was imitating Achilles to express his grief, who had twelve highborn youths killed by the funeral fire of his beloved Patroclus. Hephaestion, what started out at an attempt by both of you to create a golden age has been corrupted by your death. Alexander is mad and he would bring that madness with him if he was made Quermen."

I could not believe that Alexander had done such a thing and to dedicate those deaths to my spirit and yet I knew that Anak would not lie to me. Perhaps if I could convince them that I could control Alexander I could gain permission.

"No Hephaestion, it would not work. You would be unable to control him. I want you to promise us that you will spend some time thinking of the possible consequences should you make Alexander an immortal. He would truly believe that he was divine and in time the world would accept him as such. His thirst for conquest would never be quenched. What would happen when he really conquered the entire world? What would he do then to magnify his opinion of himself? Unlike you, or as we believe you to be, he would never be able to blend in. He would have to let the world know that Alexander the Great lives. The world would be awash in blood. Just think about it for three weeks time and if you still feel as you do we will talk about possible options and we will go to the Tribunal of Twelve with you and petition their thoughts. Will you give us your word?" Anak looked almost pleadingly into my eyes.

"You have my word." I whispered and turned away from them. I have always been an open minded person because I always prided myself on considering every conceivable possibility to any given situation. Also, these three Quermen had yet to deceive me.

Chapter Sixteen
The Decision

For three weeks I went into what the Quermen call Kanuriz, a state of deep meditation where one dwells on only one thought. Being an infant in the ways of Quermen, I was not able to stay fully in this near catatonic state for three weeks uninterrupted. The pangs of needing to feed made me aware of my weakness (I know of old Quermen who have been in Kanuriz for as long as a century without interrupting the process), but my dutiful friends supplied me with fresh blood so that I would not have to leave Habitat. The blood was so fresh that as I drank I knew the memories of the person who had unknowingly donated it. Truly amazing.

During my period of Kanuriz, I came to realize that my friends and the Tribunal of Twelve were right in their assessment of Alexander. Out of Alexander's conquests would come many golden ages and just as he desired he would so dynamically change the world that even thousands of years later humankind would be feeling the effects. But that was his legacy and a legacy is something left behind. Alexander could not live with his creation because he could never have accepted that his part in world formation would have to end. As an immortal, he would never tolerate the evolution of his creation into something new without directly overseeing it. I understood that if Alexander was to be immortalized in the way in which he wanted that he must die eventually. I would have to go on without him.

After Kanuriz, my friends came to me and wanted to know what I had concluded. I told them that they were right but I also told them that I had my doubts about being able to go through eternity without the man I love. If felt that I would never have accepted the gift if I it had occurred to me that immortality could never include Alexander. I would give it a chance and from afar I would follow my Alexander for the rest of his days. If I found separation completely unbearable, I would go before the Tribunal of Twelve and ask for the true death as an act of mercy.

Xaphaxes spoke up at this time. "There are those in the world who believe that everyone who lives comes back again. It is a sort of learning process. Each lifetime gives us something that we need and each human, no matter how inconsequential his lot may seem, gives the world something it needs. Certainly Alexander has given the world much, but he has much to make up to the world. It seems to me that if there is any truth behind this belief that Alexander is an excellent candidate to return. As a Quermen who has been so mentally linked to this man, not to mention physically linked, it could be that you will know if he is reborn. If this is truth then truth might also be that you could guide the new Alexander's life in such a way that he might find his achievements in more human friendly ways. But of course that is if this belief is truth. I don't know that there is anything after true death except blackness. I still find myself disillusioned that the gods I worshipped as king did not exist. But I suppose I needed them to be real. But if this is truth you might have something for which to wait. I know some Quermen who claim humans they were linked to have come back and some who may now be Quermen. But that is only if this belief system is true." Xaphaxes said all of this in a philosophical style making sure that I understood it was as possible to be true as it was possible to be untrue.

Suddenly I could hear cries in my mind. I doubled over grasping at the back of my skull with my hands trying to grip the pain and wrench it from my mind. This had never happened. What was it out there that could be having such a profound influence on me? Suddenly realization hit. It was Alexander. He was near death and in his dying he was screaming for me.

"Alexander is dying! I must go to him now." I started from the room but was stopped by my three friends.

"You cannot go without the Tribunal of Twelve giving permission and that is doubtful. They simply won't let you leave this early." Maneti said, his hand grasping my arm. I knew I was no match for the Tribunal of Twelve and my complete and utter desolation must have shown.

Anak spoke. "We will go with you as we promised. But you must let us speak before you say a word. Do you understand?" I nodded and the next thing I knew we were standing before these twelve very regal once-men, all of whom appeared to be in their twenties but by all accounts were of an incalculable age. How this meeting was arranged so quickly I did not know nor did I question it. I only thought of my need to be at my beloved's side no matter what I had to do.

Anak was first to begin, when all twelve Quermen nodded at us to speak our petition. "Very Revered you know why we are here before you. We petition that our mutual child, Hephaestion be granted special amnesty to go to his, all but in name, husband Alexander. That he might be with the man, for whom he lived his mortal life, at the time of his true death." I had never realized until then that these three Quermen lovers who had each given me their blood did indeed consider me their child.

"Why would we grant such a petition in light of his very words that he would give the gift to this man who we would no doubt have to destroy anyway, thereby making Alexander suffer two deaths?" Asked the Tribunal of Twelve as one thought, which we all heard in our head.

"Revered ones." Anak continued. "You have known us for millennia and we have yet to tell you anything that was other than truth. We have known Hephaesion but a short time. But in that time and even before his death when we were studying his life he never once backed out of his word once it was given. If you grant this very unprecedented request Maneti, Xaphaxes, and I will go with him to Babylon. There we will present ourselves with faces of men unknown to any there and we will be close at hand while Hephaestion speaks with his beloved and comforts him in the hour of his death. Hephaestion has given us his pledge that he will not give the gift to Alexander as he now knows the consequences of such an act. Surely Revered ones you have in your memory what such a love feels like. I have never seen anyone feel as much love for a man as Hephaestion does for this one, but he truly wants the memory of Alexander to be what Alexander had originally had as his goal and he knows that only in death will that happen."

There was but a second's pause as all twelve Quermen, in their groups of four weighed the request amongst themselves. "Hephaestion do you give us your word?"

"I do Revered ones give my word with all that I stand for. I will not give the gift to Alexander." I responded quickly and with all sincerity.

"Very well. May the fulfillment of your petition be as beneficial as you believe it will be for you and for Alexander. Now go. We await your return." As simple as that. Anak was amazing. If ever I got into trouble I would want Anak to come into court in the guise of my attorney. In a flash we had put on clothing and in the darkness at a speed that made our image indecipherable my three dads and I were headed to Babylon.

Chapter Seventeen
A Last Farewell

We arrived through the gates of Babylon as four priests from the Oracle of Siwa, with urgent news for Alexander. The magnificent city was dismally quiet as cities got in that time when great kings lay dying. When we were told how will the Shahanshah was, we assured them that our god would quickly bring him back to health as we carried a message for Alexander directly from Amun entrusted to only us to share with Alexander. We did mindplants to everyone and in minutes found ourselves in the chamber of Alexander the Great. After ridding the rooms of all the people waiting around for him die, including his hillbilly wife Roxanne and the regal Straitera, I stood there not knowing quite what to do next. It was unusual for me, one who always had a plan, to be without words.

"We will be in the shadows in case anyone seeks to disturb you Hephaestion." Maneti assured me in his soft beautiful voice.

"Thank you my friends." I said as I walked to the bedside of my beloved. His breathing was labored and he looked so unlike the virile warrior at whose side I had ridden as we attempted to conquer the world. There were lines in his face that had not been there and the wine had put a yellow cast in his skin. Much the same were those beautiful eyes, that had seemed bottomless and in which I had, on countless occasions, tried to fathom their depth, as he impaled me with his flesh. His succulent lips were parched and cracked. His chest was hardly moving regardless of the effort his breath was making to fill it. I clasped his hand in mine and leaned forward to kiss his lips.

"Alexander can you hear me?" I asked him. He made a sound and looked over. I had lost my guise so that he might recognize me. At this point it really didn't matter. Even if he lived to tell anyone that I was here it would be overlooked simply as the wishful thinking of a dying man seeing his loved one in the fever of death. "It is me, Hephaestion. I have come to be with you."

"I am truly mad. I watched my Hephaestion's funeral pyre almost six months ago. If I am mad, then insanity is my ally, if it means being with my Hephaestion." He mumbled, but he did seem to be coming round a little. I gave him a little of the tonic that Xaphaxes had given me on my death bed, while not a cure it did possess properties that made the mind more lucid.

"No my love you are not mad. I am truly Hephaestion. I have come to face death with you a final time. I was many weeks travel from here, in a land you have never seen, and even from there I heard you crying out for me." I told him, noting that he seemed to be more aware of his surroundings.

"This must be some devilish god's foul humor to play with me like this. Why torment me with my lost love? Is not my death payment enough for my transgressions?" Alexander looked up seeking answers from a higher power that probably wasn't there.

"Alexander it is really me. I have come to spend time with you. But we do not have long. I will need to leave shortly so that your generals can return. You must name the wisest of them to head your forces or your empire and all our efforts will have been for naught. Do you understand me?"

"But how Hephaestion? How can it be? You were dead for days. I was with you the entire time. I was the last to see you on your funeral pyre before it was set ablaze and your body was turned to ashes along with my heart." Alexander said to me with confusion, but I could tell he did believe me.

"It is a very long story beloved and one for which you have barely time to hear. But, no doubt, hear it you must. In brief, I caught a fever, which is almost always fatal. A healer came to see me while you were at the games, claiming to have a cure. He was no healer. For lack of a better term for you to understand he was a sort of genii, who told me he had no cure for the fever but that he could give me a gift if I chose to accept it."

"A genii, like the Persian magical creature?" Alexander asked, sipping some more of the bitter elixir. "What was the gift he offered you?

"He offered me the gift of dying and returning to life with the promise that I would stay young and never die again. I wanted to wait and talk to you about it but was advised that I did not have the time remaining." I explained at length the entire story of my death-like state and how I had been with him and Aristenes on the trip to Babylon. To reassure him that he was not being deceived I told him the words he whispered to me high up on my funeral pyre that only he would know. How my three mentors had brought me back to life and my time at the Habitat up until this very day and the special dispensation I had received to be at his side.

"Hephaestion you and I have had some amazing adventures but nothing like the one you have recently had by yourself. I wish I could have faced that one with you. I have missed you so much my eternal beloved. Each day the sunrise has awakened me only to hear my cursing the night for not taking me. The only comfort I have found is the wine flagons brought to me with first meal. My drunkenness dulls my memory and gets me through the day. At late evening I am assisted back to this chamber and before sleep once more takes me I see you sailing our boat to our secret island, just like those many years ago, and I make love to you once more. Then I curse the gods for taking you, that they might have you, and right before I go to sleep, I pray to those same gods to take my life and spare me the pain of another day. But now that is behind me. You have come back to make me like you and we can live together forever without sickness the humiliation of growing old and weak. Future generations will not be telling tales about what we did but what we are doing. We will watch each new generation be born, grow old, and die and Alexander and Hephaestion will be the one constant in their lives."

Alexander, there are no gods, there never were. We must be happy with what we had and accept the choices we made." I shook my head slowly. The words of my friends and the Tribunal of Twelve were speaking in my mind even as I looked at Alexander's visage, which had become more animated as he spoke. He was looking at me and smiling with those gloriously white even teeth. I could feel the hope draining from him as he realized the meaning behind my eyes and sad smile.

"I am so so sorry Alexander. I had thought the same thing at first. That is why I agreed to the gift in the first place, but the gift is not meant for you. It is just not meant to be."

"But why not Hephaestion? You and I would be together forever and we could rule the world! Surely you have not betrayed me too, Hephaestion. We would truly have the world and not just for a few short years."

"You have answered your own question Alexander. What you have done has greatness all over it but our actions were meant to take up but a moment of the world's history. Now the effects of what you and I did must be played out. But know that the echoes of your creation will be far reaching and still be felt when the cities you founded are but pieces of rock scattered about a shepherd's field."

"I don't believe you Hephaestion. I made a good difference in the world. Yes there were those who suffered but it was for the good that was to come." Alexander was still not convinced and I truly could not bear the thoughts of him thinking I abandoned him when I could have saved him.

"Alexander, I thought long and hard about what it would mean to give you the gift. At first I thought selfishly how it would mean that we could be together eternally without the constant fear of one of us getting killed in battle, or dying of fever, and the one remaining wait for years, perhaps, for death to reunite us. What of death my sweet king? I believe it a strong possibility that death may be the door to nothing but a dark sleep without dream. But then in my deep thought state of mind I began to see the possibilities of a world with Alexander as head of state forever. I want to show you what I saw." I reached over and lightly touched Alexander's head and for the first time as Quermen I attempted for him to see what my mind had perceived.

Within a few moments time Alexander had seen and felt the synopsis of what I had spend three weeks trying to see a way out of the final conclusion. Alexander had just fallen back on his pillow as if resigned. "That would be a world I would not want to visit on my worst enemy Hephaestion. To think that I would be the one responsible for so much suffering when all I wanted was for the world to accept each other and have the two of us as the benefactors of its prosperity and happiness. I accept your decision just as I have accepted every decision you have ever made for me." Alexander smiled and then continued," So I am back to my original lament. That you must go on forever without me and that I, according to you, must take a walk into a dreamless darkness. That doesn't seem quite fair does it?" He gave a weak half hearted laugh. The elixir was beginning to wear off and he was laboring to breathe again.

I remembered the belief of many that humans are reborn. I recited most of what Xaphaxes had told me about its possibilities. "I think my friend, King Xaphaxes, sees some merit to that belief system. He has even known some who claim to have lived before and with some good evidence, though most forget their past lives, they tend to bring aspects of them into their present life. Alexander I am going to cling to that hope and faith and I promise you that I will wait for you to come back to me. You know that I am faithful to my word. If you are somewhere reborn in this world I will seek you out and you will be mine again. At that time perhaps you can be made mine forever. There is none other than you that I want to share my existence and love with for always. It is time that I go and that you make important decisions before you also go." I leaned down and kissed Alexander the Great for the last time.

"I believe you Hephaestion and I will come to you. On that you have my word. Hold me in your arms one last time." Again I leaned over him and took him into my arms, cradling the back of his head with my hands. His lips next to my ears and I could feel the roughness of our beards rub together. "I will come back to you and be yours and we will let the world do as it will." He whispered getting progressively weaker. When I was about to lay his head back down he whispered one more time so weakly that only a Quermen could possibly have heard him.

I looked over my shoulder at him as my three friends came

out of the shadows to join me. He was watching me, a sad little smile on his face and an expression of question in his eyes. I nodded in answer and he relaxed closing his eyes. The four of us put on our priest guise and walked out the door. We ordered everyone back into the room with the knowledge that they had never left Alexander's side.

I remember thinking, "I have no doubt that he will be reborn, even if it sets a precedent in the universe. He is Alexander the Great! I just hope he doesn't come back as a female."

Chapter Eighteen
Planning for the Future

As soon as we were safely outside the palace walls we created the illusion that we were Macedonian officers and headed into a bistro where I welcomed the first glass of wine in many months. For a few minutes we sat at a private table in silence.

Xaphaxes was the first to speak. "Will you be ok Hephaestion? What you did took great strength of character. A lesser person would have failed."

"Yes, I think I will be ok. The grief is there and I think it may always be. Such an emptiness my heart feels that there are no words. He understood when he saw and that makes my heart glad. I hope now that he might rest. But friends, I have little doubt but that he will join me. When, I have no idea but he gave me his word and we never broke our word to each other. His empire will not survive his absence will it?" I stated this more than questioned it.

"No it will not. He put his emphasis on building empire not in maintaining it." Maneti said frankly as he looked in my eyes.

"Anak, did you mean what you said that night? That Alexander is a monster?" I asked him.

"Since your death he was rapidly becoming one. I said that to awaken you to reality. Hearing some of what he said to you tonight there was still a lot of human in him, but Hephaestion you complemented his soul. Without you there he was as risk of losing his humanity." Anak answered honestly as I had expected him to do.

Xaphaxes picked up the conversation. "Hephaestion what will you plan for your future? I doubt after your demonstration of faithfulness this night that the Tribunal of Twelve will insist on keeping you at the Habitat against your wishes. We three will certainly miss you but the world calls to you."

"I have not completely thought it out. But I love Egypt and its history and I think I could make a home there. Hephaestion is well known there but I can keep the guise of another indefinitely can't I?"

Maneti answered. "Yes unless something happens to distract you. Then you might lose it momentarily but those you keep close you will give a simple mindplant that can last for years. You can even create an illusion for them that will age you with time."

"That is good. I feared that I might have to go into the wilds beyond the Danube and live in abject poverty in some hut until I could safely return to the Mediterranean area years from now." I said good naturedly as possible under the current circumstances.

"You need to plan for your security." Xaphaxes said, practical as always. "I don't mean just for your Quermen body. You are a warrior and I have no doubt you will adapt and survive. I am speaking of wealth. The one with the most treasure from the earliest times is the one with the best defenses. My whole kingdom perished so I had little trouble taking my accumulated wealth along with everyone else's to hide until I had need of it. Of course, I stayed at the Habitat and never had need of it. It is still hidden where it will never be found and it is yours to use as you need it. In this instance, however, it does not hurt to think like Alexander regarding when is enough enough? You and your lover sacked the world as it were. The Shahanshah will have little use for it momentarily and he always said half of all was yours. Very shortly it will be taken by those who did nothing to earn it. I am proposing that you let the three of us help you take all that we can up to that half, which is yours by right, and we can hide it safely with mine." My three friends sat at that little round table in Babylon and waited for my answer.

"Let's do it." I said. For the next seven days my friends and I made our way into every treasury in Alexander's and my former empire, taking the best of everything. As a Quermen we were able to do this undetected. We made countless trips and each time left with loads of gold and jewels of every kind. I had to stop to feed occasionally, but other than that all was productivity.

Xaphaxes had, indeed, found a secure hiding spot. It was a remote natural cave high in what are today the Himalaya Mountains. The opening is formed in such a way that it appears not to be there to the naked eye at a distance. Once the cave is entered there are tunnels going off many different directions and there is one tunnel you cannot see at all because imperceptible to the naked eye is a rock door that takes Quermen strength to push. Once it is open the tunnel goes deep into the mountain for some miles and into a vast room, easily large enough to house a large ship. In this room when torches are lit are the treasures of many empires. Not just gold and jewelry but also the history of civilizations and the great writings of the shining lights of different ages. Since that time I have moved some of mine to various parts of the world, but the treasure of Xaphaxes remains untouched in case he or I ever have need of it.

Taking the treasure had been relatively simple. Just hours after I left Alexander he had died surrounded by his generals, who were begging him to select an heir from among them. He was fevered but held the ring, that he had always worn on his finger and which represented his power, as the greedy men raised their voices for one to be heard over the others for his choice. He had held his ring up and looked at it and smiled. "Hephaestion" he said. They reminded him that I was dead and that he must choose. With the simple words "Tear it apart." He flung the ring and he was no longer in the room. The world immediately went into an uproar as the men fought over the empire.

Alexander actually had a little known half brother back in Macedonia and the hillbilly Roxanne was due to give birth in a matter of weeks. The king's legitimate heirs, however, were given little consideration for the succession of power. Alexander had not focused a lot of attention on his unborn son as a possible heir. His body was not even cold before different accounts of his death were being spread across the empire. When reports of his death reached Greece, they were not immediately believed. Alexander's last sentence "tear it apart" was changed to "to the strongest." Yet another story said he handed his ring to Perdiccas, his bodyguard and my one time friend. Perdiccas was the obvious choice because after my death he had become a confidante of Alexander. I think that as a true friend Perdiccas initially avoided explicitly claiming power, instead suggesting that

Roxanna's baby would be king, if male; with himself, Craterus, Leonnatus and Antipater as guardians. Just as it is today, however, governing factions can agree on little. The infantry, under the command of Meleager, rejected this arrangement since they had been excluded from the discussion. Instead they supported Alexander's half-brother Philip Arrhidaeus. In time the two sides reconciled, and after the birth of Alexander IV, he and Phillip III were appointed joint kings of the Empire…albeit in name only.

Just to tie loose ends about the disposition of what Alexander and I created, I need to elaborate a little. It was not long before dissension and rivalry began to afflict the Macedonians. The satrapies handed out by Perdiccas at the Partition of Babylon became power bases each general could use to launch his own bid for power. After the assassination of Perdiccas in 321 BC, all semblance of Macedonian unity collapsed, and forty years of war between the successors ensued before the Hellenistic world settled into four stable power blocks; The Ptolemaic Kingdom of Egypt, the Seleucid Empire in the east, the Kingdom of Pergamon in Asia Minor, and Macedon. In the process both Alexander's brother and his son were murdered along with their mothers. Not long after, word reached me in Egypt that Olympia, Alexander's mother, was executed. The blood line of the greatest general ever to live was ended.

So now I stood with my three friends in the vast cavern surrounded by the product of empire.

"Our mission has been accomplished Hephaestion. We must leave this place and return to the Habitat where the Tribunal of Twelve will be waiting for our report." Maneti spoke. He was smiling and placed his hands on my shoulders.

"I need the three of you to indulge me in one final request and I will leave here with you happily." I told the three handsome Quermen, who were giving me an "Oh no, what rule do you propose breaking now?" look.

"I have just two things in Babylon that I must do. Before you ask I did not put Alexander in catosis" (which is what I had learned they had done to me to give the appearance of death)"so he will not be returning with me. It does, however, have to do with his funeral. I understand that they are not going to place him on a pyre and there are some things that I must arrange." I told them. They no doubt by now knew the futility of attempting to persuade me to do other than what I wanted.

"Very well Hephaestion. We will wait for you here so that we may return as a whole to stand before the Tribunal of Twelve. How long will we wait?" Xaphaxes asked.

"No more than seven days on the outside." I responded. I stood looking at my three handsome adopted fathers. "I have one more request which I hope you will not deny me." I thought I detected the three of them rolling their eyes.

"What Hephaestion do you want now?" All three of them asked in unison.

"I want to swallow your seed before this journey that I might carry each of you in me." I said almost shyly with my eyes downcast like a mischievous boy asking for his first kiss.

"We know you Hephaestion. You are just in want of a man." Grinned the sultry looking Maneti. They each looked at each other, laughed, dropped their tunics to the ground and stood there before me side by side.

"Perhaps." There was no point in denying it. "It has been many weeks. Longer than any time since I was but twelve. In fact, longer than any time since I died. So who wants to be first?" I asked. Anak stepped forward and placing his hands on my shoulders gently pushed me to my knees and guided my open mouth to his cock.

Anyone who has read my story to this point is no doubt well acquainted with the joys of sucking a hard cock attached to a male you enjoy. So I will not elaborate, I will leave that part of the story for you to finish in your head. Suffice it to say each of these men has a beautiful cock. Every cock is different and these are no exception. Anak's is long straight and thick, with veins that stand out. His actually looks wicked but it could not be attached to a more gentle lover. His cum is copious and tastes of oak. Next in line Maneti, the fairest of the three once-men, whose pole is very long and while it definitely has girth, is the most slender of the three once-men. Maneti's pace in my mouth is more urgent and his humanity surfaces with the sounds he makes. His muscular smooth ass tightens and his knees tend to buckle a little when he shoots his load, which is thick and ropy and tastes of berries and sugar. Last was the beautiful dark Xaphaxes. The young king was probably worshiped as much for his beauty as he was for his beneficence. His fleshy manhood is deceptive because it has such an arched curve that that it appears shorter than its nine inches. It is a darker shade of skin than the rest of his body and is nestled in blue-black hair. It is harder to suck because of its curve but in your ass it puts the receiver in ecstasy as it constantly massages the prostate. His ejaculate comes without warning followed by the sounds of his gratification and it tastes of flowery nectar.

No more had I swallowed the last of the three that I was gone and on my way to Babylon, leaving my three friends hopefully inspired to carry things further amongst themselves until my return.

Chapter Nineteen
Wrapping It Up

I was in Babylon in a very short time and took the guise of a middle-aged Macedonian diplomat. I felt this was safe since the soldiers I would be dealing with had not been home for years and further I knew that I would have better reception if I was one of their fellow countrymen. The first thing I wanted to do was check the funeral arrangements for Alexander. I was surprised he was not getting a warriors funeral and being fed to the flames. I learned that Alexander's body was placed in a gold anthropoid sarcophagus, which was in turn placed in a second gold casket. A seer called Aristander had come forth foretelling that the land where Alexander was laid to rest would be happy and unvanquishable forever. I, of course, understanding the nature of politics knew that the successors saw possession of the body as a symbol of legitimacy. I knew what I must do.

I considered Ptolemy the best of Alexander's generals and he was easy to find. He slept alone without a Persian boy to keep him warm. I made my way to his rooms in Alexander's former palace. Sitting in the bed next to him I gently shook his shoulder. Ptolemy was not a man prone to excess of drink so he aroused quite quickly to his senses. His eyes widened and he started to scream which I muted. I neglected to mention that I had taken on the appearance of Alexander. Poor Ptolemy had been aroused from a pleasant dream only to find himself in bed with his dead king. I motioned for his silence to which he agreed. I asked him many questions. I wanted to know everything from how his wife was doing running his estates back in Macedonia to the quirkiness he had confided to me about his stomach. I then got into details of how the empire had been divided who had done what and what he felt their motives were. I asked him his own motives. He told me that just as I love Egypt (thinking me Alexander) so did he and he had vied for that empire to keep it just as I wanted it. I believed him. For a general his mind was reasonably uncorrupted. I followed through with my plan. I put a mindplant in Ptolemy ordering him to steal the funeral cortege of Alexander and to take it to Memphis where it was to remain in a tomb that he was to build and be kept under honor guard always. This done I ordered Ptolemy to return to sleep but to do as I had asked or I would return and drag him to the underworld where dogs would rip out his entrails forever. He understood. I knew he would do as I had requested. To keep from boring you let me just say he followed through to the letter.

When I left the palace as a common soldier, I walked the streets for some time thinking through all I would need to do to accomplish my final task. I looked for what would be the last time for many years down the broad boulevard I took in the great palace of Nebuchadnezzar II, where Alexander and I had fucked each other senseless as we planned our new world order, it was also the place that my lovely Alexander died, and it was the place where his empire was torn apart, ironically just as he had ordered with his last words. I admired the Hanging Gardens of Babylon whose beauty was beyond description and they had belonged to me, a gift from Alexander. Next to the great temple of Ishtar stood the library, with its wealth of knowledge housed in room upon room. The great library stood tall and arrogant in its design. It was dark except for the light of one window.

I was alone. I had my three Quermen friends for which I was grateful, but I was alone with memories of a time that would soon be a memory. I decided to go to the guarded room where Alexander's gold coffin was housed and look at it one more time. I would then do what I had promised Alexander as I left his deathbed.

Yes I would do that regardless of consequences and then I would go back to my friends and I would return to Habitat to face the Tribunal of Twelve.

Conclusion

Just as I had promised the three Quermen lovers, I returned to them in seven days. They were in the cavern just as I had left them. They looked at me in amazement and with a flash of dread in their eyes.

"Are you ready to face the Tribunal of Twelve?" I asked them, ignoring the look they were giving me. "No real sense to put your robes back on as I imagine we will head straight to the Habitat." I said jovially, attempting to ignore the look of disapproval I was getting from all three.

We arrived at the Habitat in good time. All the way there I was receiving questions from Quermen Three as I had decided to name them. They advised me repeatedly on what and what not to say to the Tribunal of Twelve. I was given strict orders to allow Anak to speak first. Almost immediately upon arriving, we were summoned to council chambers. As we walked before the Tribunal of Twelve, I felt the icy stares of twelve sets of eyes focused on me.

"Most Revered Tribunal of Twelve," I said with an even proud voice. "Permit me to introduce Aristenes, my adopted son and a new member of Quermen."

The End

www.ingramcontent.com/pod-product-compliance
Lightning Source LLC
Chambersburg PA
CBHW070453260626
47161CB00004B/1291